SHIVER

Alex Nye

Kelpies

In memory of my parents,
Barbara and Ken Gollaglee.
Much missed. Never forgotten.

Kelpies is an imprint of Floris Books

First published in 2009 by Floris Books
This second edition published in 2014
Second printing 2016

The publisher acknowledges subsidy from
Creative Scotland towards the publication
of this volume

 This book is also available
as an eBook

British Library CIP data available
ISBN 978-178250-150-3
Printed in Poland

*"...this is how all our stories begin,
in darkness with our eyes closed,
and all our stories end the same way..."*

Lemony Snicket

Old Territory

Samuel and Fiona looked back at the house. It rose above the trees, its many windows gleaming in the fading light. Dunadd was a great draughty building, with winding corridors and dark passageways. Samuel had never lived anywhere quite like it before. He and his mother rented a small whitewashed cottage from the owners of the estate, which sat just across the courtyard from Dunadd House, with only a few plum trees and a white stone archway between the two.

Fiona lived in the main house, along with her mother and two brothers, Charles and Sebastian. She had lived here all her life. Things had improved since Samuel had come to stay in the cottage. For a start, she had a friend now, someone her own age, who could defend her against her brothers.

Chris Morton, Fiona's mother, lived nervously in the house, with some reluctance. Ever since her husband had died here when the children were small, she'd felt a shadow hanging over the house, but she had never felt able to leave Dunadd. It was their home, after all. Mortons had lived here for generations. The fact that Isabel Cunningham lived in the cottage across the way helped matters to some extent; it eased the loneliness, for the two families often spent companionable evenings together, in the huge upstairs drawing room.

Samuel's mother, Isabel, was an artist – or a sculptor to be more precise – and used one of the barns as a studio. She had cleared it out, fitted new worktops, whitewashed the walls and transformed it into her own personal space. She was often buried away in here, creating weird and wonderful objects which she then attempted to sell. They didn't fetch an awful lot of money; she and Samuel were always struggling, leading a hand-to-mouth existence, but he was used to that. It didn't bother him, particularly.

In fact, he felt rather special, living up here on Sheriffmuir. It was so wild and remote. None of his mates at school could boast anything quite as extreme as this. His mother had been delighted to move here, because the rent was so ridiculously cheap after their flat in Edinburgh, and it was just what she wanted; somewhere to paint and sculpt and a place where Samuel could stretch his wings. Isabel constantly reassured herself that they were not completely isolated; there were three other children for Samuel to hang about with. The fact that he had not exactly hit it off with Charles and Sebastian was neither here nor there. They would ... eventually. Boys always did. Didn't they?

Christmas was looming, and they were anticipating more blizzards, like last year.

"Will it be as bad, d'you think?" Samuel asked.

"Nah," Fiona reassured him. "Last year was different. It was out of this world. It'll snow, but not *that* badly."

Samuel remembered the ten-foot snowdrifts and how they'd been unable to leave the moor for days. Even Granny Hughes and her husband, who worked on the estate during the daytime, had been unable to return to their centrally-heated flat in the town. They'd had to stay up here with the rest of them.

"D'you think your mum still misses your dad?" Samuel asked, out of the blue. He was walking along beside Fiona. They could see the clustered rooftops of Dunadd, poking out from between the skeletal trees.

"What made you ask that?" Fiona said.

He shrugged. "It just occurred to me, that's all ..."

"It's so long ago now ... since he died, I mean. I don't really know if she misses him or not," she replied, thinking about it properly for the first time in ages. "She must do, I suppose. It's funny, but I hardly remember him."

Samuel nodded, but said nothing. He knew what

that felt like. He couldn't remember his father either. The only information he had gathered about him was that he had acquired another family somehow and preferred to keep his distance. He knew, of course, that there must be more to it than that, but all he had ever known was his mother. And when you didn't know any different, well ...

He sometimes longed to be part of a big family: security in numbers, that kind of thing. People who could say to each other "C'mon you guys" or "come along team." He had heard other mothers using expressions like that in a rather smug way when they rounded up their offspring after school. He didn't really want his mother to be like that.

"It must be hard for you, too," Fiona said.

Samuel shrugged. "It's no problem. I'm used to it."

"Still, at least we've got friends." Then she added, "I just hope Mum never decides to move ..."

Samuel glanced at her quickly, noticing the worried frown.

"What makes you say that?"

"I don't know. It's just ... well, sometimes she floats these ideas. But I don't think she means it."

"I hope not," Samuel said.

"She couldn't do. Anyway, race you back to the house?" she cried, then set off at a run before Samuel had a chance to realize what was going on. She leapt over fallen branches and spreading tree roots, but her race came to an abrupt end when she finally stumbled in a rabbit hole, which sent her crashing onto her back.

"You alright?" he asked, bending over her, but she shrieked with laughter, flinging her arms up either side of her head. Last year's leaves were stuck in her short spiky fair hair.

"What am I like?" she cried, laughing at herself.

"An idiot," he said, helping her up. "That's what you're like."

"Mum says I'm getting too old to go charging about the place like this."

At twelve years old, you were supposed to *act* mature even if you didn't feel it. But Fiona was a free spirit. She'd always lived out in the countryside, far away from other houses and people and she was used to doing her own thing; she didn't really care what others thought about her. Samuel liked that about her. It was refreshing, especially when girls at school were so preoccupied with the way they looked and dressed, standing in tight semi-circles with their arms folded, passing judgement on everyone else. Fiona wasn't like that. She was, in many ways, a tomboy.

From the studio, they could hear the whirr of a power tool.

Samuel looked sceptical. "I wonder what Mum's up to now?" he mumbled.

He decided he'd better go and light the stove in the cottage before his mum realized it had gone out again, otherwise they'd freeze tonight.

"What does she need a power tool for?" Fiona said, half laughing.

"Goodness knows."

"We could go and see?" Fiona suggested, but he shook his head. He knew to his cost what it meant if he disturbed his mother at work. No, it would be better if he just got on with making his own tea. Beans on toast, again.

"Have tea at ours tonight," she suggested.

Samuel shook his head. He secretly enjoyed the peace and quiet, when the cottage was empty, dark and cold. He liked the moment before he switched the lights on, staring out at the mist in the trees with the brown hills of Sheriffmuir beyond. It reminded him of how lucky he was to live here.

"Suit yourself," Fiona said lightly. "I'll see you tomorrow then."

"Yep!" He nodded and smiled, then watched her stroll happily away across the courtyard. Once she'd gone he pushed the door open and stepped inside the gloomy cottage.

The Night Plays Tricks

The cottage was quite cheerless. No lights on. No fire lit. Samuel went out to the barn and heaped a load of dirty coal into a bucket, then cracked some kindling. He'd have the stove roaring in no time. It could be a bit sluggish, and both he and his mother had been known to lose their tempers with it on occasion, but they had more or less got the hang of it now.

Soon a warm welcoming glow emanated from its heart, although not quite enough to remove the raw edge from the air. He switched on a lamp or two, then started to make something to eat, wondering if he should take some through to his mum in the studio. If she was feeling inspired she could be at it for hours. He didn't mind, because he knew what she was like. But occasionally she lost herself in her work.

He inspected the empty fridge gloomily. They needed to go shopping again. He switched the TV on and ate beans on toast.

The winter evening closed in until a fat yellow

moon appeared through the branches of the trees, illuminating the world outside. Samuel stood with his elbows on the high window ledge and looked outside at the courtyard and the woods beyond. He loved that view. It was so peaceful; he could even hear the sound of water nearby, the murmuring of the Wharry Burn, an ever-constant presence in his life now.

Going outside, he followed the path to his mother's studio. The power tool was silent. Pushing open the big barn door, he called out, "Mum? You in there?"

"Oh, Samuel. What time is it?" his mother asked.

"'Bout sixish, I think."

"Sorry. I had no idea. I've been busy ... as you can see."

He glanced at the mess around the place. There were wood shavings all over the floor and the work surfaces were cluttered with objects. Where, in all of this, was her work of art? Then he saw that she had been fashioning something out of wood ... a strange shape.

"D'you like it?"

"Um ... yes," he offered, although he didn't really know what to make of it. It certainly looked like the kind of thing that people in art galleries would buy and position in a spacious window or hallway as a centrepiece for other people to look at.

"I love working with wood," she enthused in a slightly tired voice. "And the great thing is, there's so much of it here."

"Did you make it out of fallen stuff from the woods?" he asked.

"Yep," she said proudly.

He looked at it contemplatively. Samuel liked drawing and sketching, and for a moment he wondered if his mother would show him how to use tools and make things out of wood. She seemed to know what he was thinking and patted his shoulder.

"Maybe I'll give you a lesson," she said quietly. "You *and* Fiona. Have you had anything to eat?" she added guiltily.

"Beans on toast."

"Sorry about that. I'll do a nice roast tomorrow. How about that?"

He nodded. "Sounds good ... but we need to go shopping first."

"So we do."

As they crossed the courtyard to the cottage, she looked up at the sky thoughtfully and said, "I suppose I'd better get plenty of food in tomorrow, in case it snows."

Darkness fell across the two separate households. Lights were extinguished, fires burned low and heads lay sleeping on pillows. But they were not alone.

Other things lurked in the shadows, biding their time, waiting. Dunadd was full of *other* presences. Silent presences ... that had not yet made themselves felt.

The moon still shone brightly in the night sky, but the wind had picked up. In her bed that night, Fiona heard it whistling in her bedroom chimney, as it blasted the sides of the huge old house and bent the trees as it swept across Sheriffmuir. It was the voice of her childhood. She was used to it. Without it she would be lost. But it tended to drown out other, more suspicious sounds: strange creaks and murmurings in the corridor outside her bedroom door. So no one suspected or noticed that there was movement in the air. Was that a light pattering of footsteps? No one saw the eyes burning in the dark. Fiona turned over and went back to sleep, lulled by the roar of the wind.

Across the courtyard Samuel also lay and listened. The wind banged at the windows, rattled the doors, threatening to tear the odd roof slate off. Earlier the moor had seemed so still when he went to the barn to fetch his mum, but now everything had changed. The trees were full of it, creaking with the strain.

Samuel was just drifting off to sleep when a scream pierced the night. He sat bolt upright, instantly awake, senses alert.

What was that?, he thought, his heart racing.

In the woods just beyond the cottage, a rabbit had been caught by a stoat. It was the scream of a dying animal, that was all. Nature simply having its way. But Samuel didn't know this.

The night was playing tricks on him again.

The Tapestry

The next morning Samuel's mother prepared to set off in the car to get some provisions in before it started to snow.

"Good idea," Chris Morton had agreed, when she heard, so the two women left together, determined to make the most of it and have a coffee at the same time.

"Might as well ... while we're down in civilization," Mrs Morton said.

Isabel, who had spent too many hours working away in her studio the day before, was only too glad of the opportunity to take a break.

Samuel watched them drive away, then wandered next door in search of Fiona. He found Granny Hughes on the stairs, struggling manfully with the Hoover.

"I'll take that upstairs for you, if you like," he offered.

"Aw no, I can manage," she said, grabbing it firmly by the neck. "I'm used to it. You're a good lad," she gasped, glancing resentfully in the direction of Charles and Sebastian who were lurking at the foot of the stairs. "You put the others to shame, so ye do."

Charles glowered sulkily, but Sebastian had the good grace to look embarrassed.

"And don't be giving me any of yer filthy looks," she called after them. "I can't be doing with it."

Charles sloped off, the shadows of the corridor swallowing him whole.

Granny Hughes shook her head sorrowfully. "I never can mind what's up wi' that lad. He's like his father was before him. A gloomy soul ... "

"D'you remember him?" Samuel asked.

She looked at him then for the first time.

"Of course I remember him. It was a sad day when he died. This house has never bin quite the same since, that's for sure," and she nodded her head sadly. "Plug this in for me, there's a good lad," she added, once she'd wrestled the Hoover onto the upstairs landing. Samuel pushed it into the plug socket and switched on.

Immediately, Granny Hughes began to bump the machine over the painfully thin carpet that covered the bare boards. It was a carpet that had seen better days. There was nothing Granny liked more than a good clean and her facial expression assumed a level of severe satisfaction as she chased the dust about the house, moving it from one room to another.

Samuel left her to her business. He found Fiona up

in the drawing room on the wide window seat. He sat down beside her, without saying anything.

"Did you hear the wind last night?" Fiona asked him.

He nodded.

"Funny, because it was so still earlier."

Samuel noticed that the door to the library, which was situated to the right of the huge stone fireplace, stood open.

"That's unusual!" he remarked, almost to himself.

"What?" she asked.

"It's usually locked."

"Oh, that!" Fiona sounded unconcerned.

The room had always been strictly off-limits. Fiona's mother, Chris Morton, didn't like anyone going in there. She seemed to have a thing about it – unsurprisingly, as it was the room where her husband died. For that very reason, it had always intrigued the children, particularly Samuel. The books in it were old and musty and it always seemed to contain an air of secrecy. Fiona was more reluctant to go in there. It reminded her of how sad they had all been when they had first lost their father. She didn't want to think about that right now.

Samuel had no such qualms and wandered in, then stood looking up at the closely-stacked shelves.

"What are you doing?" she asked anxiously, from outside.

"Just looking, that's all. Your dad had so many books, didn't he?" he added, as Fiona came and stood beside him. "Who reads them?"

She shrugged. "Whoever feels like it." Then she added in a small voice, "No one really."

"What's that?" Samuel had wandered over to a far corner of the room and stood looking up at a framed tapestry on the wall. He peered closer. The work was delicate, the stitches very fine and its great age evident by the faded look of the linen, which was distorted and worn smooth in places.

"I think *she* did it," Fiona said.

"She?"

"Catherine ..."

Fiona pointed to the initials embroidered in the corner. CM.

Last year, they had found the diary of Fiona's ancestor, Catherine Morton, in the attic, and had uncovered her tragic story.

"It's funny how you can live with a thing for so long that you take it for granted in the end and hardly notice it."

The wooden frame was burnished and marked with the passing of the years, "genuinely distressed" as antique dealers would say. Samuel studied the little sampler and felt again the familiar sense of intrigue gripping him. The design contained a tower, with a boy and girl standing beside it, holding hands. It was recognizable as *their* tower, the tower attached to Dunadd House where the boys' bedrooms were situated, and where Granny Hughes and her husband slept if they were staying over, although Granny preferred not to. She was afraid to sleep there at night.

They both stared at it for a long time.

"I wonder who the two children are supposed to be?" Samuel asked, studying it.

"At your detective work again, are you?"

Charles's dark tousled head appeared round the door.

"Charles!" Fiona gasped. "You made me jump!"

"Sorry. Anyway, what are you two doing in here?"

"Just looking!" Samuel was quick to reply.

Charles gave him a concentrated look. "I know you two. You don't give up, do you?"

"What?" Samuel said, trying to look innocent.

"You know ... this place might *seem* like a museum to you, but it *is* our home."

"He knows that, Charles," Fiona cut in. "Don't be so rude."

"I'm not being rude. I'm just reminding our friend here that this isn't a theme park."

"I never thought it was," Samuel said.

"It's a strange old house," Fiona sighed. "Even you have to admit that, Charles."

"Of course I do."

"Look at this," she added, pointing at the tapestry. Charles peered closely at it.

"What about it?" he said. "It's always been there."

"I know," Fiona added, "but like Samuel says ... who are the children in the picture supposed to be? And why did Catherine Morton stitch them into her tapestry?"

Charles glanced at her quickly. "How do you know it was her?"

"Isn't it obvious?" She showed him the initials in the corner.

Charles nodded slowly. "Oh yeah ... I guess you're right. I'd never really looked at it before."

"I was just wondering ... that was all," Samuel broke in.

"Curiosity killed the cat," Charles remarked, as they all walked out of the library into the huge drawing room beyond.

"This place has so many secrets," Samuel sighed. "Doesn't it ever drive you mad?"

Charles shrugged. "I don't think about it. Some of

them we will find out ... and others will remain a mystery, I expect."

"What makes you say that?" Samuel said.

"He's looking for inspiration," Fiona cried. "He's writing a ghost story for school, aren't you, Charles?"

"Are you?" Samuel asked him.

"Private, thank you very much." Charles shook his head dismissively. "Got to run. Things to do."

Fiona and Samuel watched him disappear up to the tower, taking the stairs two at a time. His room lay at the top, far away from prying eyes.

"Lucky devil," Samuel said, watching him go.

"Why?" Fiona glanced at him.

"Well, wouldn't it be cool to have a bedroom at the top of a tower?" he added. "Honestly, Fiona, you take this place for granted sometimes."

"I suppose I do," she replied, but she was looking vague and distracted again. Samuel knew that look.

"What is it?" he asked, waiting for her to elaborate. He knew she would, eventually.

"Well," she began. "It's just ..."

"Just what?" he prompted.

"That tapestry," she went on.

"What about it?"

"Well, it's got me thinking. Do you remember the entry in Catherine Morton's journal?"

"Which one," he murmured.

"The one that was pinned open at the museum, in Edinburgh ... the day we went to visit?"

"What about it?" He waited.

"They thought she was a witch, because she heard voices," Fiona explained. "You know ... she wrote about hearing a boy and girl laughing and quarrelling. Remember? The noise used to wake her up."

"But what's that got to do with the tapestry?" Samuel looked baffled.

"Don't you see?" she cried, exasperated. "The boy and the girl in the sampler? Perhaps they're the same ones as in Catherine Morton's diary. Perhaps *that's* who she heard?"

"Just so long as *we* don't start hearing anything ourselves," Samuel said.

Their voices grew fainter as they wandered away down the passage.

Although the children didn't know it, eyes were watching them from the shadows, listening to their voices as they whispered about their problems. Up in Charles's room someone waited ... had always been waiting.

Chris Morton had sometimes suspected that Charles was adversely affected by the house, and now and again aired the idea of moving from Dunadd altogether. She suspected that her son's dark moods were more than teenage hormones, but perhaps it was all in her imagination. After all ... he was getting to a difficult age and fourteen-year-old boys were known to be unpredictable and secretive in their habits.

This is what she told herself.

On the landing below, the grandfather clock ticked in the silence: a comforting familiar sound.

The Secret Staircase

It was thoughts of this tapestry and the two figures in it that prompted Fiona and Samuel to start looking. They wanted to know who the children were. While Charles was away upstairs in his tower room, writing his precious ghost story, they wandered round Dunadd ... searching for clues.

"Samuel, what exactly are we looking for?" Fiona asked, as she followed him about the dark passageways of the house, trying doors and opening cupboards.

His head reappeared from a broom cupboard, a cobweb draped across the top of it. "I don't know."

"You've ... er ..." she pointed to the top of his head.

He pulled the sticky cobweb off and flung it to the floor. "Place could do with a clean," he remarked.

"Don't tell Granny that," Fiona said. "Anyway, you're poking in places where we don't normally go."

"That's the point! We're looking in places where *nobody* usually goes ... where anything could have

been hidden away, without anyone knowing about it."
Fiona looked sceptical and fed up.

After taking a break for lunch, Samuel made a decision. "D'you know what ...? I think we should go back to the library."

"What for?"

"Because that's where all the problems seem to begin and end in this house."

Fiona shrugged and trotted after him, glad that Charles couldn't see them now. He would be sure to have something to say about them conducting their own investigation.

They pushed open the library door. Shelves of books towered to the ceiling. Samuel scanned the room with his eyes for any clues. On one of the bookshelves stood a marble figure, the head and shoulders of some stuffy-looking Greek philosopher.

"Plato," Fiona explained.

"Who?"

She shrugged. "He's a Greek philosopher. That's all I know. And for some reason we have a bust of him. Or rather ... Dad did."

Samuel raised a tentative hand and explored it with his fingertips. He had the briefest fantasy that a touch of the sculpture would impart some magic knowledge to him, and set them on their way to finding the answers to their mystery. But no such luck. The marble bust just sat there, looking slightly pompous and hideous.

"Ah well." Samuel turned his back on it, sighing deeply. It was then his eyes fell upon the massive stone fireplace, set into the side of the wall.

"Big fireplace that, for a room this size," he commented.

Fiona nodded.

"Especially as it's never lit," she added.

Their eyes met. "It's funny," Fiona said, "but now you mention it, I've never noticed a chimney on this part of the house."

"Maybe it shares the same chimney as the drawing room?" Samuel said. "That's why you can't see it from outside."

"That's not possible, is it?"

The two of them approached the fireplace together, and peered up into the darkness.

"Blocked!" Samuel concluded.

"Or, like I said ... no chimney."

"A false fireplace you mean?" he asked.

"But why?" Fiona shook her head in bewilderment. "I mean ... I suppose it could have just been decorative ... but it seems a bit pointless."

"It's an old house," Samuel shrugged. "Someone must have had their reasons. Plenty of them, probably."

He was standing *inside* the fireplace now, feeling around the back of it with his hands. One of the stone slabs seemed to give slightly.

"Fiona," he gasped. "Look at this."

She crouched down, bumping herself on the old servants' bell as she did so. Samuel pressed again upon the loose stone slab. Both of them watched in amazement as a section of the fireplace moved aside to reveal a dim passageway and a staircase leading up into the gloom beyond.

"Wow! This is amazing," Fiona breathed softly. "I never knew this was here!"

Samuel turned to look at her. "What else don't you know?"

As they bent to examine the opening more closely, a rush of cold air washed against their faces and they shivered.

"It's freezing in there."

"Where do you think it goes?" Fiona asked.

"Well, I think we're about to find out." Samuel was about to step into the darkness, but Fiona stopped him, her hand on his arm.

"Wait ... we need a torch first."

She rooted around in her father's old leather desk, then produced a flashlight, switching it on and off to test the battery.

"Seems okay," Fiona said and handed it to Samuel. "Right. You go first."

"Why me?"

"You're a boy. You like taking risks." She pushed him in front of her.

The two of them began to climb the steep narrow steps, with the help of the searchlight.

Fiona gave a wistful glance back at the entrance. She could just make it out below them, as the darkness swallowed them whole and they left the light far behind. What if someone came into the library and closed the secret staircase off again, not knowing they were in here? They might remain here forever. Her blood ran cold at the prospect. It was a risk they would just have to take. She decided not to mention her fears to Samuel. There was no point in making both of them nervous.

"Where d'you think it comes out?" she asked instead, as they climbed.

The staircase turned an abrupt corner and opened out into a low passageway.

"We must be above the drawing room now," Samuel replied.

"Try not to make any noise," she added. "We don't want anyone below to hear us."

The way twisted and turned and soon it was hard to

work out exactly which part of the house they were in anymore. They felt like mice, scurrying about behind the wooden panelling.

Eventually they came to a dead end.

"What's the matter?" Fiona asked, peering over his shoulder.

"We can't go any further," Samuel said.

"But we must be able to," she insisted, disappointment flooding her.

He shook his head. "This is the end, I'm afraid."

"Where d'you think we are?" Fiona breathed.

Samuel hazarded a guess. "Somewhere up in the tower, I'd guess. The walls seem to be either brick or stone here." He rapped on the side of the passageway with his knuckles. Some of it sounded hollow and gave off an eerie echo.

"But why has it been blocked off?"

"I don't know." Samuel was at a loss. "What a find, though. Can't wait to tell the others.

"Maybe we should start heading back," Fiona murmured, still concerned by the thought of being trapped in there, forever.

It seemed to take an age to find their way back again and, for Fiona, the sight of daylight at the bottom of the narrow stone staircase was a huge relief as she had started to feel claustrophobic.

"Phew! Am I glad to be out of there!" she gasped, as they burst back into the library.

Samuel wasn't listening. "We've found a secret staircase. How brilliant is that?"

But Fiona was staring at something over Samuel's shoulder.

"What is it?"

She shook her head, trying to formulate the words. She had just seen – or thought she'd seen – a small, dark, shadowy shape sweep past the open doorway; so fast she wasn't even sure she'd seen it at all. But it left her with an inexplicable *feeling*.

"Hello?" Fiona called, walking slowly towards the entrance to the drawing room. "Is anyone there?"

"What *are* you doing?" Samuel began. Fiona put her finger to her lips.

"Sssssh!"

Silence. Then ... a child's laughter. As faint as a breath of air. Hardly discernible.

"Did you hear that?" Fiona whispered hoarsely, spinning round to face Samuel.

He nodded. "It could have been anything."

"Charles or Sebastian, you mean? I don't think so," Fiona said.

"Then what do you think it was?" Samuel asked nervously.

They looked at each other.

Anything was possible in this old house. Maybe they *had* found Catherine Morton's laughing children.

Charles's Story

In his bedroom, up in the tower, Charles glanced at his computer screen. It was switched on, but he hadn't been near it in hours. He sometimes liked playing computer games, or downloading music from the internet onto his iPod. One of the games he played followed the adventures of a boy trapped in a haunted house, who had to find his way out of a maze of passageways. Like all computer games, it was repetitive and unsatisfying in the end, but he liked it and played it obsessively, to the point where it almost became a fixation. He was also trying to write his ghost story for school, but it wasn't going very well. Fiona had put him off with her comments.

It could be so boring in the school holidays with no one but his brother and sister to hang about with ... apart from Samuel. Fiona had taken to him and the two were as thick as thieves. Part of him envied his sister for having a friend she could confide in. Charles was a loner. He didn't confess his secrets to anyone.

Not even to his brother, Seb, who had the room next door.

He stared out of the window at the grounds and garden below, turning when he heard a light tapping noise on the keyboard behind him. On the blank computer screen had appeared one sinister little word.

```
Hello
```

That was strange. He moved closer, peered at the screen, then pressed the delete button. It was an instinctive reaction – an attempt to remove the evidence, erase it. Words didn't appear of their own accord like that. Had he been typing earlier and left something on the screen? A computer could hardly produce text all by itself, no matter how amazing modern technology might be.

"That's weird," he said to himself. His voice sounded uncannily loud in the silence of the enclosed space. His room was quite small, without much furniture in it, apart from a bed, the computer desk, a bookcase and a wardrobe. He liked it this spartan. He didn't need much.

On an impulse he sat down on the chair, and typed in the words:

Hello to you, too, whoever you are.

"Stupid," he muttered out loud. He pressed the delete button again, and watched the sentence disappear, swallowed up by the cursor.

Then he swivelled about on his chair and wrote a fresh sentence, beginning with the title of his story.

SHIVER. A ghost story.

He liked that. He'd made a start. Now – he stared thoughtfully at the window – he needed an atmospheric sentence to begin with: something that would make readers' spines tingle.

The snow began to fall steadily,
blanketing the hills in silence.

Too wordy? he wondered.

Oh, it's not too bad, he told himself. *In fact, it's fairly promising.*

He turned back to the computer screen, his fingers on the keyboard, but his cheeks suddenly drained of colour. From out of the screen drifted a face, its features assembling themselves before his eyes as if from smoke.

He blinked his eyes.

Was he imagining things? He shook his head to clear it of any fuzz. The face slowly faded out again, as if it had never been there.

How could that be? He reached out a hand and touched the computer screen. Smooth and cold to the touch, like porcelain. Nothing there. An electric buzz emerging from the back of it. That was all.

Surely writing a ghost story couldn't summon up a real ghost, could it? That was absurd. Completely bizarre. *I mean, I know my English teachers tell me to use my imagination,* he thought, *but this is taking it a bit far.*

"If this is some kind of joke," he muttered, "then it's not very funny." There was no way he could carry on writing his ghost story now.

He made for the door and bolted downstairs.

After he'd gone, the empty room seemed to let out a faint exhalation that was almost a sigh. A shady figure emerged, hovering near the window. It drifted slowly towards the computer and blew onto the screen. The opening lines of Charles's ghost story vanished from sight.

Charles found the others in the kitchen.

"Where's Mum?" he asked.

"Gone shopping," Fiona told him. "With Isabel. House to ourselves."

"Oh!"

"What's up?"

"Nothing," he mumbled.

"Charles, you're white as a sheet," she persisted. "What is it?"

"You've not been trying to write your ghost story again, have you?" Sebastian teased him.

"How did you know?" he snapped, glancing quickly in Fiona's direction. For a brief moment Charles wondered if his brother had had anything to do with the hazy face he'd seen drift from the screen when he was writing. Perhaps Sebastian had done something to his computer? He was a bit of a technical whizkid. *Yes, perhaps that was it,* he thought. *It was just some kind of elaborate hoax.*

"Wait till you hear what we've found," Fiona burst out, not giving Charles time to think about his problem any further.

"What now?" he sighed, taking on his older brother's stance. He slid into a seat next to them at the kitchen table, trying his best to look tolerably bored.

"A secret staircase!" she cried. She nodded her head furiously. "Honestly! We've found a secret staircase in the library!"

"Fiona, calm down," Sebastian said.

"But it's true!"

"Have *you* seen it?" Charles asked, looking straight at his brother.

Sebastian shook his head. "Not yet."

"What did Mum say about it?" he continued.

"She doesn't know yet. Come on. We'll show you."

Fiona leapt up from the table and began to lead the way past the grandfather clock and up the spiralling staircase. The house waited ... and watched. Every unopened door seemed to contain a secret and the clock itself began to chime, its notes resounding as far as the tower itself.

Samuel was a little reluctant to show the other two what they had discovered. He wasn't sure what they would make of it.

In the library, all four children stood before the fireplace.

"And?" Charles said. "Now what?"

"Wait," Fiona whispered. "Come on, Samuel ... help me." The two of them leant into the back of the fireplace and began to feel around for the loose stone slab. Nothing happened.

Fiona's face fell. "It worked last time ... didn't it, Samuel? We pressed this slab here and ... maybe we're not pressing it hard enough. How did it work before?

Maybe there's a catch ..." She felt about desperately with her fingers, eventually slapping the stone with the flat of her palm in frustration.

Charles and Sebastian looked sceptical.

"I told you," Charles said, leaning back and folding his arms in satisfaction. "A couple of regular detectives you make. Still, if it keeps you happy, kids."

Fiona glowered at him. "It's true ... isn't it, Samuel? It was right here."

Samuel nodded. "She's not making it up. I was there. We pressed something and the wall slid back and there was this staircase. It lead up into a passageway."

Charles and Sebastian were looking at Samuel, half-mocking. His voice trailed away. There was no way they were going to believe him without evidence.

"How can we prove it to you?" Fiona said. "And why won't this thing open?" she cried, slapping it again, hard. Her hand went red with the impact and she shook it in pain. "Ouch!"

"So," Charles said. "Where do you think this secret passageway leads?" He hid his curiosity beneath a thin layer of sarcasm.

Samuel looked him straight in the eye. "Up to the tower, I think. Somewhere near your room."

Charles blanched all of a sudden.

A secret staircase and passageway, leading to his

own bedroom? First, a smoky face drifting out of his computer screen, now this? He was beginning to feel unnerved.

"What's up?" Sebastian asked him.

"You've not been messing about with my computer, have you?" Charles asked his brother, point-blank.

"No. Why would I do that?"

Charles searched Sebastian's face. He didn't know whether to believe him or not.

Fiona and Samuel were still investigating the back of the stone fireplace, apparently unable to accept that it wasn't responding to their efforts this time. Charles sighed. Perhaps there *was* a secret passageway, lurking at the back there somewhere. His mother was right. This *had* always been a strange house to live in.

"It's all very well for Mr MacFarlane down at the Lynns Farm, or the landlord at the Sheriffmuir Inn, to tell stories," his mother had often said in the past, "but we have to get on with things. This is our home."

Exactly, thought Charles. *We have to get on with things.*

"Well, I wouldn't rush to tell Mum about your non-existent discovery just yet," he said sarcastically, as he headed reluctantly back up the stairs to his room, leaving the others to their own devices. He had made up his mind. It was time he got back to his computer once and for all, and if a face materialized in front of him this time, he'd deal with it. He'd unplug the wretched thing and demand to know what Sebastian had been doing to it.

Up in his bedroom everything was just as he had left it. But the opening sentence of his ghost story had been deleted. He pressed the cursor once or twice, to scroll down the page, but there was nothing there. *Oh well, he'd just have to start again.* He was beginning to feel in the mood this time. All this talk of secret staircases had given him a few ideas.

Broken Vases

It was Saturday night, and in the drawing room a bright fire burned in the large stone fireplace. Chris Morton and Isabel had come back from their shopping expedition, tired and weary. At least now the larder and fridge at the cottage were well-stocked. *No more beans on toast for a while,* Samuel thought. He and Fiona had been thinking about the secret staircase they'd found, and wondering why it hadn't opened a second time. It was so frustrating. The others simply wouldn't believe them, but there was nothing they could do to convince them. And Charles had been right ... there was no point in telling their mothers just yet.

Mr Hughes wheezed as he dropped more logs into the huge basket beside the hearth.

"Thank you, Jim," Chris Morton smiled. "That'll keep us going."

"Aye, you'll need it alright," he murmured. "It's going to be a cold one."

"Help yourself to a whisky in the kitchen when

you're done," Mrs Morton added. There was no fear of Mr Hughes forgetting to do that. He liked a glass of malt at the end of the day and there was no crime in that, he mused – although Mrs Hughes might have something different to say on the subject.

"When's your mother coming over, Samuel?" Mrs Morton asked, glancing in his direction.

"Soon. When she's finished in the studio, I think."

Isabel had dived into the studio after tea to try and do a bit more work on her wooden sculpture and to tidy up the clutter from the day before. She could never keep away from her work for long.

Fiona was sitting at the piano, looking bored and fidgety, running her fingers along its closed lid.

"Fiona ... rather than playing it like that," her mother said sarcastically, "you could actually open the piano and try playing it properly! At least it would make me feel all those expensive lessons have been worth it."

"Can't be bothered," Fiona said, and sloped off to join Samuel in the window seat.

"Now you're just *trying* to be difficult." Chris Morton rolled her eyes and wondered for the hundredth time what she had done wrong, and what on earth she would have done without the support of her new friend, Isabel Cunningham. She had been unsure about Samuel's influence on her daughter at first, but he'd grown on her. Besides, Fiona seemed to like him and the two were almost inseparable. All she wanted was harmony within her family, without all the tensions and conflicts that had been brewing since Samuel arrived. She was aware that Charles, in particular, disliked Samuel. Had she made the right decision, she wondered, encouraging them to live here?

But it was better than being alone on Sheriffmuir, wasn't it?

The old house seemed to creak and groan around them with some deep buried awareness.

Charles appeared in the doorway, looking agitated. She recognised that look; it meant that something was bothering him … but, of course, being Charles, he wouldn't admit it.

"What have you been up to?" his mother asked.

"Nothing."

"Working on his story, probably," Fiona said.

"What story's that?"

"Just a ghost story," Charles cut in, sheepishly.

"What's it called?" his mother persisted.

He hesitated. "I thought I might call it *Shiver*."

"Oh." She wrinkled her nose slightly. "Sounds promising. I'm impressed, Charles. Just hope it doesn't give us all the shivers. We have enough of those already. Come and get warm," she coaxed.

It was a tradition that on Saturday nights the family would gather by the fireside. The two older boys seemed reluctant to join in nowadays, but their mother still insisted on it. It was a way of keeping the family together.

In the window seat, Fiona glanced down at Samuel's notepad. He was always sketching and drawing. At every available opportunity he would take out his pencil, sharpen it to a precise point and conjure up an image with a few sharp lines.

"What's that?" she whispered, tilting her head to one side.

He turned the pad to show her. It was a cross-section sketch of the fireplace in the library next door, with the back of it removed to reveal the secret staircase they'd found lying behind it. Fiona nodded, but said nothing.

"Your mother's taking her time," Mrs Morton commented.

Samuel instinctively covered his drawing with one hand and glanced out of the window into the darkness.

"Perhaps I'd better fetch her," he said, although he made no move to do so.

The moor had been swallowed up by the night. Outside the tall trees in front of the house were shapeless masses, teased by the wind. His mother would be in her little workshop in the old barn, clattering about, trying to organize the mess that was her studio. She was never really aware of what was going on around her when she was in that place. He wouldn't like to be out there now, in the dark with no lights on. She'd have her torch with her, of course, so why was he worrying anyway? *She was big enough to look after herself,* Samuel told himself, *and she was perfectly safe. There was nothing on this moor to be afraid of.*

"Ah, that's her now, I think," Mrs Morton said, hearing footsteps below. Suddenly there was a dull smashing noise downstairs. They all looked at each other.

"Are you alright?" Chris called, moving towards the door.

They waited to hear Isabel cry out, "Oh yes, I'm fine. Sorry about that. I tripped and crashed into something."

But Chris Morton's call was met with silence.

They all went out onto the landing, expecting to see Isabel below, but there didn't seem to be anyone there. At the bottom of the staircase was a broken vase, shattered into several pieces on the hardwood flooring. Mrs Morton went down and picked up the broken shards in her fingers.

"That's strange," she said. "How did that happen?"

"I think I'll just go and check on Mum," Samuel said. Something made him want to reassure himself that she was safe.

"I'll come with you," Fiona began.

"No." Samuel rounded on her more sharply than he'd intended. "You stay here. It's cold outside."

Out in the courtyard he could see a light in the barn. His mother must still be inside. He went closer and pushed the heavy door open.

"Samuel?" She turned and looked at him, smiling. He sighed with relief. She looked as right as rain. Why had he feared that something terrible might have happened? He was being silly. One broken vase did not amount to anything serious.

"Everyone's waiting for you upstairs," he told her. "Chris was hoping you'd come over."

Isabel sighed and scooped a handful of shattered glass into a dustpan.

"Something must have got into the barn earlier," she muttered.

"What d'you mean?"

"A few things have been broken."

"Like what?"

"One or two pieces I'd been working on. I hadn't finished them yet, but there's no point now."

Then he realized that broken glass was scrunching under his feet like biscuit crumbs.

"Who would have done that?" he cried, feeling ready to accuse anyone. He could be highly protective of his mother at times.

"Don't look so alarmed. It was probably a fox maybe, or a mink."

"That smashed up your work?" he said, incredulously.

Isabel shrugged. "It's possible. At least my wood carving's still okay. Come on," she added, turning her back on the mess. "Let's go next door. I'm starting to enjoy these evenings together, aren't you?"

He nodded. "Just so long as Charles isn't too grumpy."

"Just ignore him," she said. "He can't keep it up forever. No one can. And Sebastian's alright with you now, isn't he?"

"Suppose."

"There you are, then."

They walked out into the cold night, shutting the door of the barn behind them.

Isabel turned up in the drawing room wearing her scruffy overalls and a big knitted grey cardigan that was one or two sizes too big for her. No one seemed to mind. They were all very comfortable with each other by now.

"All quiet on the Western Front?" Mrs Morton asked

her cheerfully, by way of a greeting. It was a phrase she used a lot, although her children didn't really know what it meant.

"Oh, is that for me?" Isabel said, helping herself to a glass of red wine on the coffee table. "Just what the doctor ordered."

"What's this?" she added then, noticing the remains of a delicate porcelain vase lying on the sofa beside Chris Morton.

"It fell and broke just a few minutes ago, at the bottom of the stairs. No one was near it or anything."

"How odd."

"Mmm." Chris Morton seemed to dismiss it from her mind as she said, "Come and join us. Jim has filled the basket to the brim and I've decided I'm going to toast myself tonight." She stretched her feet towards the flames.

"Toast! Now there's an idea," Fiona cried.

"Go on then … But organize it yourself," her mother threw over her shoulder. "I'm too tired to move. And someone call Sebastian, will you?"

"Come on, Samuel," Fiona said, and pulled him after her.

Down in the kitchen Fiona flung open the fridge and searched for the butter dish, then grabbed a loaf from the bread bin.

When the fridge door slammed shut, Samuel was looking at her.

"What's up?" she asked. He was looking preoccupied and worried.

"My mum's studio was wrecked. Some of her things were broken ... a couple of new pieces she's been working on. She's not too bothered and thought it might have been a fox or something ..."

"I wonder what it was?"

"Who knows."

"You don't think it was Sebastian, do you?" Fiona exclaimed.

"Why him?"

She shrugged. "Well, he's the only one who wasn't in the drawing room at the time. And you heard what Charles said to him about his computer ... asked him if he'd been messing about with it."

"But why would he do that?"

"I don't know," she said. "I'm just trying to find some rational explanation."

They moved about the big kitchen, collecting the things they needed.

"Unless ..." Samuel hesitated "... it was something else."

"Meaning what?" But Samuel was already heading back up the stairs and did not reply.

Upstairs, the two women were comfortably ensconced in armchairs either side of the huge fireplace, engaged in adult talk.

"And then what did he say?" Mrs Morton was asking, all concerned.

"Oh, it's all such a long time ago now ... What does any of it matter?" Isabel quickly changed the subject when she saw her son enter the room. Samuel was used to this. His mother often had intimate conversations with other women about "the past," which were instantly cut off as soon as he reappeared.

Fiona knelt down on the rug with the loaf before her.

"Where's Sebastian?" her mother said. "Hasn't he come down yet? Charles, go and call him, will you?"

Charles went to the landing and called his brother's name.

Fiona fixed a slice of bread to the toasting fork and held it out to the flames. So began the ritual. Hot butter melted off the slices of toast and dribbled onto their fingers. Once Sebastian had joined them as well, it would have looked a comfortable scene to any outsider. Two adults and four children gathered beside a roaring blaze, making toast, their faces bathed in orange firelight while the rest of the room around them remained mostly dark. A winter scene. A cosy scene. But one which hid an uncomfortable truth and lots of dark secrets.

Charles held out the toasting fork to Samuel in a rare show of friendship. Samuel hesitated, then took it.

"Do you ever miss your old friends in Edinburgh?" Charles asked him unexpectedly.

Samuel nodded. "Sometimes. I still keep in touch, by email and things."

Isabel had overheard them and interrupted. "We're going to have one of them to stay one of these days, aren't we, Samuel? If I can ever get myself organized enough."

"Yeah. They wouldn't believe all this. But I miss the city sometimes," he added.

"There must have been lots to do," Charles said quietly, as if he was trying to imagine a different life for himself.

"There's lots to do here, as well," Samuel said.

"It's hard, making new friends," Charles murmured, as the conversation of the adults faded out again.

"Tell me about it," Samuel said wistfully.

The hours ticked by and the fire burned low in the grate. Granny and Mr Hughes had left some time ago, leaving the kitchen scrupulously tidy and the tea towels hanging up to dry. Granny, despite her complaints, was like a ministering angel, leaving cleanliness and warmth in her wake. Isabel was falling asleep in one of the armchairs, wrapped in a plaid blanket, her feet curled beneath her. Chris Morton was gazing into the fire, thoughtfully, looking relaxed in the company around her. On the walls, portraits of former Morton ancestors – people who had owned this house in the dark and distant past – stared down at the group clustered by the hearth. They seemed to be judging, offering opinions, while at the same time withholding comment. Samuel liked these portraits, even though they also unnerved him. Dark probing eyes followed him about the room. He liked the sense of history, of things having happened here before: mysterious things; dark and secretive things. The weight of its history could also be oppressive. The Morton children certainly found it to be so at times.

Down below the grandfather clock began to chime midnight.

"The witching hour," Chris Morton murmured. "Time for my beauty sleep."

Isabel raised her head, looking bemused.

"Where am I?" she mumbled.

"You're next door, Mum."

"Of course. That means I've got to go out into the cold," she groaned.

"Never mind, Isabel," Fiona said. "You've got your son to help you," and she nudged Samuel playfully.

As the great room emptied itself, eyes watched them from the shadows. Fiona was nervous, thinking about the secret staircase they'd found. She was sure she'd seen something earlier out the corner of her eye, after they'd emerged from the gloomy exit hole in the fireplace: a swift, dark shape. Where had the passageway led and why did it suddenly stop? Why had it been blocked off? What was it hiding? And who or what had broken the vase in the hallway downstairs? Was the same person responsible for wrecking Isabel's studio?

Fiona's head buzzed with unanswered questions. It would be hard to get to sleep tonight.

In the cottage next door, Samuel was thinking along similar lines. He opened his notebook and flipped through the pages. He'd been busy tonight. Sketch after sketch appeared: some of the secret staircase and the library fireplace, from all sorts of angles; one or two of Charles and Sebastian. He'd even copied some of the portraits on the walls. Last of all, he'd drawn the tower with the two children standing beside it, just as it appeared in the tapestry sewn by Catherine Morton all those years ago.

Who were the children? he wondered, staring at his own sketch.

What other secrets did this ancient house contain?

Ghost Girl

Upstairs, Charles's room waited for him. *Shiver, the ghost story*, hadn't made a great deal of progress. Someone or something kept interfering with it. Nervously, he switched the computer off at the wall to stop the intrusive buzzing that was coming out the back of it. Instantly the thing went dead. Charles passed a hand in front of the screen, experimentally. Nothing there. Then he peered into it and saw his own hazy reflection looking back at himself, his head distorted into a weird bulbous shape by the glass.

It was late ... and he was tired. He climbed into bed, thinking wearily about the strange day he'd had. *What had all that nonsense been about a hidden staircase in the back of the fireplace? Was there anything in it? Or were they winding him and Sebastian up?* He decided he'd have a look for himself ... tomorrow.

He rolled over onto his side and stared at the wall. He was just drifting off to sleep when a sound caught his attention. He opened his eyes. What was that?

Something was being shifted about in the next room. There was a bang, then a muffled bump.

But there *was* no room next door. Not on that side anyway.

He sat up and pressed his ear flat against the wooden panelling. There it was again. As if someone was moving furniture about.

He tapped on the wooden panelling with his knuckles. Once ... then twice.

Immediately the movement next door – if there *was* a next door – stopped.

His eyes grew wide in the dark.

He waited for a while, to see if the noises would start up again.

Then he was sure he heard voices ... whispering.

"He has heard us!"

"Sssh. Do not make a move."

"It is too late now. He knows that we are here."

"Good. I am glad of it. 'Tis time they were made aware."

Two children; male and female.

Charles rapped lightly on the wooden panelling again and the voices instantly fell silent. Not a single murmur.

"I know you're there," he called out, feeling brave. "Whoever you are."

Absolute silence. Whoever was listening had decided to go to ground.

I'm going to sleep now, he said to himself. He punched his pillows into softly billowing shapes and flopped down again.

I'm going to talk to Fiona and Samuel about this. He couldn't help thinking about their elaborate story about a hidden staircase. *But surely this was just his imagination running riot. He had gone to bed extremely late, after all, and he was exhausted.*

Oh, great! he thought. *I'm really losing it now ... and hearing things.*

He thought fleetingly about going to wake Sebastian up, but he was just so tired ... and what would he tell him anyway? In another minute or two he'd be sound asleep, noise or no noise.

But sleep completely eluded him, despite the lateness of the hour. He lay awake, worrying. Eventually he gave up, struggled out of bed and went in search of his brother. He tapped on Sebastian's door down the hall.

The muffled sound of someone moving beneath a duvet reached his ears. "What is it?"

Charles needed no further invitation. Pushing the door open, he leant against the door jamb. Sebastian looked at him, perplexed.

"Did you hear all that noise?" Charles asked.

Sebastian looked at him blankly.

"What noise?"

"You must have heard it? Through the wall ... movement ... and dragging."

Sebastian shook his head.

"Voices?" Charles added, hopefully.

Sebastian stared, his face impassive.

"Charles, I think you need to get some rest. You're seriously beginning to worry me."

"It's true. Honestly. I'm not imagining it."

"Are you sure you're not getting just a teeny bit carried away with your ghost story?"

Charles glared at his brother resentfully. "Fine. Don't believe me then!" His disappointment was evident.

Sebastian hesitated a moment.

"I ... I don't know what to think," he muttered, embarrassed. "I really don't." Then he sighed heavily and added, "I know Fiona and Samuel believe in all this ghost nonsense but, to be honest, I don't ... not really."

"Well how can you explain what I just heard?"

"I can't," Sebastian said.

"Exactly. And it wasn't you who heard it. It was me. And I know I'm not lying."

"What you *thought* you heard ..." Sebastian corrected

him, sleepily. 'It's late. Talk to Fiona and Samuel about it in the morning.'

"Yeah, right," Charles scoffed bitterly, turning his back on his brother.

Sebastian rolled over and within minutes was asleep again, his dreams undisturbed.

Charles shook his head, wishing he could sleep as soundly.

Outside, tiny snowflakes floated down in the darkness, landing on the outstretched branches of the trees. Chris Morton and Isabel had done the shopping just in time. An eerie silence descended over Dunadd. Fiona lay sleeping in her big four poster; Mrs Morton, propped up against mountainous pillows, read a book until her eyelids drooped; and Sebastian lay sleeping, untroubled by the day's events. Even Charles fell asleep eventually, unable to keep his eyelids open a second longer.

"Hello!"

He leapt up, sitting bolt upright in bed.

A voice had spoken to him in the darkness, as clear as a bell, right beside his ear.

"What the ...?" *Was this some kind of trick?*

He groped around for the light switch. In his panic a pile of books and magazines slid off his bedside table, landing in a chaotic heap on the floor.

When he finally found the lamp, he realized it wasn't going to oblige; the electricity obviously wasn't working ... or the bulb had gone again. It was always playing up, but its timing was abysmal. He stared around him fearfully.

Gradually his eyes grew accustomed to the dark and he could make out the dim shape of a figure sitting on the end of his bed, staring at him.

He froze. The hair on his scalp stood on end and his blood seemed to stop moving around his body.

It was a child. She was dressed simply in a stained, grey shift; her hands and face were very pale, and her hair and eyes were as black as coal. She was inspecting him as if he were an object of curiosity. There were huge shadows under her eyes.

He stared at her for a long time before summoning the courage to speak.

"Who are you?"

"My name is Eliza." Her voice was tinkling and clear, but there was a hint of mischief behind the dulcet tones. She giggled.

"Eliza?" he repeated stupidly.

She nodded. "That is so. I live here."

"You ... live here?" Again he found himself repeating her words, as if to arrange them in his own head.

She giggled again: a wicked laugh that sent shivers down his spine.

"It has been a long time. We have been sleeping."

"Sleeping?"

"My brother and I," she murmured, leaning forward slightly. "But now you have woken us. You and your friends."

"My friends?"

"The boy and the girl who were in the library earlier, looking at us in the tapestry. They who found the secret place at the back of the fireplace. They are your friends, are they not?"

"Sort of," Charles mumbled. He was still in shock and was finding it difficult to form a coherent sentence. "She's my sister."

"And the boy?"

"That's Samuel. He lives in the cottage next door."

But why am I telling you this? he thought. *You're not real. You're a figment of my imagination. This is definitely a dream. You're...*

The child peered at him curiously. "I wish to thank you for waking us."

Charles leant as far back from her as he possibly could. She smelt funny. There was something musty and decrepit about her and there were traces of some powdery substance on her body, as if she'd been doused with something.

"My brother will not come out," she said, shaking

her head slightly as if in despair. She was very neat and trim and held her little hands folded in front of her, like a doll. But a doll with haunted eyes and a look of neglect about her hair and clothing.

"He is afeart," she finished sadly.

Charles screwed his eyes up anxiously. "Afraid? What of?"

"Oh, everything," she sighed.

He's afraid, Charles felt like blurting out. *How does she think I feel?*

"And your name is?" she asked.

Charles stared at her. "Charles," he whispered, in a hoarse voice. "Charles Morton."

She opened her eyes wide. "We share the same name, you and I. We shall be seeing more of each other, I believe."

Then, incredibly, she held out her narrow little hand to be shaken. Charles backed away. Her fingers looked so brittle, almost skeletal, and he recoiled from the very idea of touching her. It was too creepy to even consider.

"You will not shake hands with me," she stated, as if it was a fact. "How very rude of you."

She put her head on one side, studying him in the gloom, as if he had offended her. Then he stared in horror as she picked herself up and walked sedately towards the wall, vanishing through the wooden panels, as if made of nothing more substantial than air and smoke.

Charles leapt from the bed, and pressed himself flat against the panelling, listening for any sound.

"Come back," he shouted.

But she had gone. And all the distant sounds of furniture being shifted about, the muffled bumps and thuds and the whispered voices of before had disappeared as well.

Just wait till I tell the others about this in the morning, he thought. Then he wondered how on earth he would begin to describe what had just taken place, without making himself sound like a raving lunatic, especially as Sebastian seemed disinclined to believe him.

Charles's Problem

It had snowed during the night, but not quite enough to make the moor inaccessible. The trees were heavy with it and it had gathered against the outbuildings and the barn. Charles looked out and blinked his eyes.

Then he turned to stare at his bedroom wall. Had he dreamt that visit from the ghost girl last night? Eliza Morton. Who was she? And why was she here? He couldn't wait a moment longer. He threw on his clothes and knocked on Sebastian's door.

His brother looked sleepy.

"Conference. Downstairs," Charles announced.

"What?"

"Five minutes," Charles added. "I've got something to tell you all."

"Has this got anything to do with last night?" But Charles didn't answer him.

Sebastian shrugged and rolled his eyes. As far as he was concerned, it was too early in the morning to get worked up about anything. He fell back lazily against the pillows. Another five minutes wouldn't hurt ...

"Are you feeling alright?" Fiona asked about an hour later, looking at her brother with concern.

"No, I'm not," he said. "You're not going to believe what I've got to tell you. That secret staircase you were on about yesterday ...?"

Fiona and Samuel stared at him, wondering what he was about to say next.

"I think we should take another look at the fireplace," he announced.

"Why?" Samuel said.

"What do you mean why?" Charles repeated, flabbergasted.

"I mean, it's a good idea and all that. But why now? You didn't want to know yesterday."

Charles took a deep breath. He had to try and describe the events of last night, even if they laughed in his face.

"Last night ... in my room," he began, "I heard all these strange noises through the wall." He could see Sebastian looking at him sceptically, but he blundered on, undeterred.

"First of all, it was just like things being moved

about, and then I heard voices. Two children ... a boy and a girl."

Fiona glanced at Samuel.

"Then it stopped and I fell asleep," he went on, beginning to lose the thread a little, "but later I woke up and there was this girl sitting on the end of my bed. She was really small ... for her age I mean."

"How d'you know how old she was?" his brother asked, quizzically.

"I don't ... but she was much younger than us ... and she didn't look at all well."

Sebastian let out a short, sharp laugh.

"I know it sounds a bit crazy ..."

"You can say that again," his brother said, releasing a slow whistle. "Your ghost story is really freaking you out!"

" ... but it's true. I'm not making this up!"

"Sebastian, be quiet and listen to what he's got to say," Fiona snapped.

"She said her name was Eliza," Charles went on. The others gave him their full attention now, their faces rapt.

"She thanked me for waking them," he finished. "She said that we'd woken them up ... Or something like that."

There was a long silence.

"How did we do that?" Fiona said softly.

"By finding that secret staircase?" Samuel wondered aloud.

"But how?"

No one knew the answer to that. Even Sebastian had grown quiet. He was looking less blasé about it all. It was beginning to seem as if his brother Charles was telling the truth. Strange things had been known to happen in this house before. Why not again?

"So, what are we going to do about it?" Fiona said.

"First up, we're going to find that secret passage," Charles said. "I bet she'll be back. She practically promised she'd come again."

"Oh, that'll be nice," Sebastian quipped. "Did she say when?"

"Sebastian, stop being stupid and help us look," Fiona ordered, marching off in the direction of the stairs.

"Where are you going?" the others called.

"Back up to the library. There must be a way to make that passage open up again."

In the library the Morton ancestors stared down from their elaborate frames, watching the passing of history once again. They watched everything from their lofty position and made no comment. What was there to say? Another adventure was occupying the children: another mystery in need of a resolution. The house would only give up its secrets reluctantly. The Morton ancestors knew this.

The marble bust of Plato sat on the shelf, its blank eyeballs offering up no wisdom. Fiona and Samuel immediately began feeling around at the back of the stone fireplace, knowing beforehand that it was hopeless.

"It's stuck," Fiona breathed. "It just ... won't ... budge ..."

Charles joined them, but Sebastian stood aloof from the proceedings, shaking his head. He leant slightly against the wall, accidentally pressing the old servants' bell. No answering bell jangled in the bowels of the building, however. Instead, something else happened. One of the stone slabs at the back of the fireplace began to move aside ... just like last time ... with a heavy grating noise.

"What did you do?" Fiona cried.

"Nothing," Sebastian said. "I just ..." he looked dumbfounded and pointed to the servants' bell on the wall.

"So that's it," Samuel laughed. "One of us must have knocked it last time without realizing. Well, we'll know next time."

"Well, I like to do my bit," Sebastian murmured.

"Come on ... don't just stand there," Charles

instructed everyone. He disappeared inside the passage and began to climb the staircase. They used the torch again, running its beam over the old stone walls. It smelt so dank and fetid. No fresh air had reached this place for what seemed like centuries.

"I wonder what they used it for?" Fiona said. "In the old days, I mean."

"A priest hole?" Charles suggested.

"What's that?"

"You know, when Catholics were persecuted and run to ground. Some old houses had a secret place to hide in. They called it a priest hole."

"Or it could be for other reasons," Samuel added. "In any house as old and isolated as this, you'd want to have somewhere to hide from your enemies, just in case."

"That's true," Sebastian said.

"Or ..." Fiona began to elaborate, "it could just lead to a room that was closed off for some unknown reason."

Samuel, tuning in to her train of thought, added jokingly, "where two ghostly children live."

Charles stood still, horrified. "What ...? Until we woke them?"

"Look, I'm going back downstairs," Sebastian said, feeling suddenly spooked by the conversation. "One of us needs to make sure the coast is clear."

"Chic-ken," Fiona sang in a high-pitched, sing-song voice.

"I'm just being sensible, that's all."

"He's right," Samuel said. "We wouldn't want to get trapped here. Suppose someone closed the entrance by mistake, not knowing we were in here?"

"That's what I thought last time," Fiona admitted, "but I was trying hard not to say anything."

"Exactly ... so I'll just shuffle along, back downstairs," Sebastian said.

"D'you need the torch?" Charles called back over his shoulder.

"I'll manage," his brother replied.

"Good. I wasn't going to give it to him, anyway," Charles added, as Sebastian disappeared. "We need it ourselves."

They bent their heads low as the passage twisted and turned.

"See, here? This is where I think we come near to the tower," Samuel said, tapping Charles on the shoulder.

"You could be right."

They went as far as they could, until they came up against a blank wall like last time. They tapped on it.

"Maybe there's some way of opening this?" Fiona suggested. "Maybe it's not a wall at all ... but an entrance. Like the fireplace downstairs."

"How would we know?" Charles said, shining the torch into every crevice and crack before them.

Samuel took a penknife out of his pocket, and began sliding it between the joints in the stone brickwork. Nothing. Again, they'd drawn a blank.

"Blast!" Fiona cried out in frustration, and rapped her hand against the wall.

Immediately they heard some kind of shuffling going on behind it. Muffled voices.

They stood still and listened. Charles recognized the familiar sounds. They were the same as he'd heard the night before. This time, they were more muffled, because they were coming from beyond a brick wall, instead of behind wooden panelling.

"That's what I heard last night," Charles exclaimed, turning to the others, his eyes bright with excitement. "Maybe we're right next to my bedroom in the tower. And perhaps, if we can't get into the sealed-off room from here, there's a hidden entrance in my room too. After all, it's only wood panelling. Not stone, as far as we know."

"We've got to tell Mum about this!" Fiona cried.

"What on earth for?" Charles asked in surprise.

"Be sensible!" Fiona hissed. "We can't exactly *not* tell her about this hidden staircase, can we? It's too exciting."

"I suppose you're right. But she doesn't need to

know about the noises ... or the fact that we think there's a secret room somewhere," he added. "You know what she's like. She'll go into one of her tailspins again." Fiona grunted in agreement.

"Sssh, you two," Samuel whispered. He was leaning with his ear against the cold stone wall. A small terrified child's voice could be heard beyond.

"Come away, Eliza, please," it whined. "I like this not at all."

"They are out there," another voice replied. "Just on the other side. I know 'tis so. I can hear them."

"*Please*, Eliza," the other begged. "Please come away. You will draw them towards us."

"Shush now. There is no need to be afeart."

"But I am, Eliza. I am. I want our mother."

There was a pause, as if the boy was afraid at having spoken the words out loud.

The other voice sounded chill and hostile now.

"You know that is not possible. Do not speak of her again."

"But Eliza ..."

Then they heard a soft whimpering, of a child crying. It broke Fiona's heart to listen to it. It sounded so forlorn.

Oh please, someone, comfort him, Fiona thought, inside her head. But she didn't dare say it out loud.

"They will help us," Eliza said.

"Who will help us, Eliza?" He sounded so afraid, so timid.

Fiona turned to the others, her face white as a sheet. "They're talking about *us*," she breathed.

"How can we possibly help *them*?" Samuel added, gazing at his friend. Their faces were lit only by the gleam of the flashlight.

Charles was running his hand over the rough surface of the blank wall in front of them.

"We helped last time," he murmured softly. "Perhaps it's time to do it again."

The other two stared at him, aware of the implications of what he was saying. Once again, they had found themselves involved in something beyond their understanding. And perhaps beyond their control.

Trapped in Time

"I must get an electrician to fix this problem," Chris Morton was complaining, as she pressed the switch on and off.

"What is it?" Granny asked her. "Lights gone again? I tell you, this house has a mind of its own, so it does. I'll warrant the wiring's dodgy."

"I could get Jim to take a look at it," Chris suggested hopefully. That would be one less thing to worry about, if he could fix the problem.

"I wouldn't bank on it, if I were you, Mrs Morton," Granny said in a sour voice. "Wiring's not his thing."

"Oh well, I'll get someone else then. At some point," Chris Morton murmured vaguely. "Oh look ... it's back on again," she added in surprise, as the kitchen light decided of its own accord to switch on after all, flooding the dim room with light.

"That's better," Granny Hughes declared. "I can see better to cook now. Just as well. I don't want to end up putting one of the pets in the pot."

"Granny, really," Chris Morton said, and chuckled slightly. "I don't think Fiona would forgive you if you did."

"She should keep that rabbit in its cage then, so she should."

Chris Morton whisked the said rabbit into its cage, just to be on the safe side and moved it away into another room.

"Fiona?" she called. "Come and see to this rabbit, will you?"

"Yes, Mum. Just coming," a distant voice called from upstairs.

"What are they up to now, I wonder?" Chris Morton said.

"Goodness knows," Granny added, in her dour tones. "I wouldn't like to hazard a guess. You'd have thought they'd have wanted to go out in the snow ... get the sledges out ... or their skis. It's certainly deep enough."

Sebastian stood alone in the empty library, waiting for the others to reappear. He felt really foolish, not to mention sheepish. He should have listened to his brother's anxieties the night before. Guiltily, he recalled how Charles had stood in his doorway, long after they should have been asleep, claiming he'd heard voices through the wall. It had all sounded so ludicrous at the time. And now here they were ... finding hidden passages and stairways leading into unknown and unseen depths of the house, almost as if there were two worlds contained within the one. He wished he hadn't been so dismissive of Charles last night. It had created tension between the two brothers, unsurprisingly. Sebastian had effectively accused him of lying or, at the very least, of imagining things, as if he were deranged or untrustworthy. He wondered how he could make it up to him.

He could hear noises coming from the hole in the fireplace. The others were returning.

"How did you get on?" Sebastian said, as they emerged from the hole in the back of the fireplace.

"We got so far, then ..." Charles began.

"A dead end," Fiona finished for him. "But we heard the voices Charles talked about. We could hear them clearly on the other side. They were talking about us."

Sebastian looked surprised and shuffled his feet awkwardly. "I guess I owe you an apology," he muttered, without looking at his brother.

Charles shrugged. There was a small silence while everyone took this on board.

"What were you supposed to do, anyway?" Charles conceded. "It did sound a bit weird, I suppose."

"A bit?" Sebastian couldn't help exclaiming. "This is getting seriously creepy," he added.

"I know ... isn't it amazing?" Fiona cried.

"That's one word for it," he said, not sounding quite so convinced as his sister.

"Anyway, Mum's calling me," Fiona said. "I'd better go."

"Yeah ... and we've got to tell her about this passageway. It's so cool!"

"My mum'll love this too," said Samuel.

They tidied up the library a bit, then all rushed downstairs to tell Mrs Morton and Isabel about their discovery.

Meanwhile, in a hidden unseen part of the house, Eliza Morton sat surrounded by dust and debris. There was grey powder on the boards all about her, which hadn't been disturbed in years. Across the floor were scattered some broken toys. Ruined books spilled from a damp bookcase and a fat spider scuttled over the mottled pages. It was a dank, gloomy place, which no light had penetrated in years. No child should have had to remain here for long. But these two children had.

Eliza looked across at her little brother.

He sniffed sadly to himself, wiping a thin, bony wrist across his face.

Eliza had no patience with him. Finally, growing bored, she moved towards the wall and drifted through the cracks to the other side.

Her brother looked up to see her vanish. "Eliza, come back," he wailed. "You must not go to the other side."

But she could no longer hear him. He was all alone in the silent shadowy "other place" that no sane person would ever want to visit.

Mrs Morton and Isabel were shocked to learn that the children had been probing about again, into matters that were best left undisturbed. Granny Hughes certainly didn't like the sound of it at all and said the children had no business to be meddling. Isabel was a bit softer in her prognosis.

"I suppose it keeps them out of mischief ..." she murmured absently, in that vague way of hers. "A bit of detective work around an old house like this! If I was their age, I'd be at it too. In fact, I think I'd find it irresistible."

Granny Hughes rolled her eyes, so that no one else could see. *What were these women like, with their fancy ideas and their artistic leanings,* she thought to herself sourly. "Lives with her head in the clouds, that one ..." she muttered under her breath, but again, no one heard her ... which was just as well.

"So ..." Mrs Morton sighed, getting up wearily from where she was seated at the table. "Let's have a look at this secret entrance of yours. Just so we know what you're talking about."

The adults followed the children back up the stairs, through the drawing room, and into the library at the far end ... the very room Chris Morton had always feared. Now here they were, staring at another unresolved mystery, one she had never suspected. A secret staircase, hidden behind a dummy fireplace; a fireplace she had never questioned the existence of. She had always known it had been blocked, but had never understood why, until now.

Granny Hughes had decided to remain in the kitchen. She had no desire to join in the fun and antics of the others. It was difficult enough trying to dust, clean and vacuum great draughty rooms, without finding out there were secret openings all over the place, leading to goodness knows where. No thank you. She preferred to do a bit of baking, leaving the others to their fanciful notions.

Upstairs, Isabel, Mrs Morton and the four children stood in front of the great yawning stone fireplace ... so much larger than the room really warranted, in spite of its high ceiling, although this had never occurred to any of them before now. The library was a fairly narrow room, relatively speaking.

Isabel approached it gingerly. "So, where do you think it opens ...?" she asked, peering closer.

Fiona was there before her. "We didn't know how we got in at first. Samuel and I were just looking and then a stone swung open at the back. We couldn't work it out. Then Sebastian made us realize ..."

"It was an accident, really," Sebastian added sheepishly.

"He leant on it by mistake," Fiona cried, excited.

"Leant on what?" Chris Morton asked.

"The old servants' bell. Here! Look!" Fiona pressed the big black button set into the plaster on the side of the wall. Immediately, a grating noise was heard and a stone at the back of the fireplace began to slide sideways.

Isabel and Mrs Morton stared and stared.

"Fantastic, isn't it?" Fiona cried.

"Fantastically creepy," Sebastian muttered.

"How ... amazing!" Isabel murmured, stepping forward and gazing into the gaping void. "It's a wonder the tourist books don't mention it."

Chris Morton was looking less thrilled by the discovery. "How could they if we didn't even know it was here?"

"What is it, d'you think?" Samuel asked. "What was it used for?"

"We thought maybe a priest hole?" Fiona offered.

In all the excitement Charles remained quiet. He was the one, after all, who had suffered the closest contact with the mysterious intruders that apparently lived in the walls of the old house. However, the Morton children had wisely made no mention of this at all ... Nor of the voices they had heard and the suspicions they harboured. They were too concerned about their mother's negative reaction to it all, and the idea that she would insist on a house move. None of them wanted that.

Mrs Morton went to the back of the fireplace and inspected it closely. "I think you're right ... it must be a priest hole," she decided. "I can't think what else it would be. There were plenty of them. I just didn't know we had one here. It's odd though. Did you say there's no actual room or cubby? Just this staircase?" The children nodded. "Usually if a priest wanted to be hidden, he'd have an entire little chamber to hide in, complete with candles and books, a pitcher of water, some bedding maybe and other necessities. Where does the staircase go?"

Although she asked the question, she didn't really want to know.

"It just goes on and on," Fiona said, "up through the house. We think it ends in the tower."

"Let's investigate, shall we?" Isabel suggested eagerly.

Chris Morton shuddered again. "I really don't want to, to be honest." The thought of all that unknown darkness, with who knew what lurking there, wasn't something that particularly appealed to her ... but she didn't want to let the children know that.

Isabel glanced at her friend sympathetically. "I suppose you've been through enough in this old house of yours," Isabel said. "But we ought to check it out ... make sure it's safe. D'you want me to go first?"

Mrs Morton rallied. "No, no ... we'll all go together."

They trooped up the secret staircase, along the pitch-black passage overhead; groping their way forward in the gloom, bumping into each other noisily and making quite a commotion. Fiona and Samuel hoped they wouldn't come across anything significantly weird that would lead Mrs Morton and Isabel to suspect there was any reason to pack up and leave the house. Surely, with this much commotion, any ghosts lurking here would have made themselves scarce long before, chased away by all the noise.

"Ouch!"

"Was that someone's foot?" Mrs Morton apologized.

"Yes, mine," Charles offered grimly.

"Can you just mind where you're putting your elbow, Samuel," Isabel grumbled.

"Honestly, you grown-ups are so noisy," Fiona laughed. "We were *much* quieter on our own."

"Well, it's not easy ..." Isabel breathed, labouring along. "We're not as young as you lot."

"Or as brave," Fiona added.

"That's a matter of opinion," Isabel said.

"If we're less brave," Chris Morton qualified from the back of the line, "it's because we know more."

Finally, after much bickering and stumbling, they got to the end of the dreary passageway, and the adults rapped on the hollow-sounding bit of the wall.

"D'you know what I think?" Mrs Morton said, shining the flashlight at the brick wall before them. "I think Charles's bedroom is behind here, and this is maybe an old entrance to it."

"But why? And what for?" Charles asked.

His mother shrugged. "No idea, but all of this is making me uneasy. Let's get back downstairs. I need some fresh air."

Night Wanderings

After the discovery of the secret staircase, everyone felt a little nervous at Dunadd. Fiona sat in her room, on her four-poster bed and stared out of the window at the impenetrable dark. The power had failed again – it did this almost every night now – and a few candles glimmered on her mantelpiece.

"You be careful of those," Granny had warned. "They're dangerous. Don't want this place going up like a torch."

Her mother, Chris Morton, didn't like the idea of them all having candles in their own bedrooms, but what else could they do?

Fiona glanced towards the window again to see if it was snowing, but let out a small gasp. A face was staring back at her through the window.

After the initial jolt of shock, she gathered her wits about her. *It's your own reflection, silly*, she told herself sternly. Bravely she stood up, walked towards the window and made as if to wipe the glass. Her fingers froze on impact and she pulled them away automatically. It was not her own face she could see hovering there ... she was sure of it. It was that of another ... a little girl, grave and pale. She gazed at Fiona for a long painful moment with sad, grey eyes. Fiona was too frightened to scream ... or to call for help.

She stood still and watched the image fade as if it had never been there at all. Outside it had begun to snow again, gentle flakes drifting down through the ebony sky.

Fiona tried to breathe some life back into her frozen fingers. Why was the glass so cold?

The face at the window had vanished, but could she trust her own senses? What had she really just seen?

Turning back, she realized that she *could* see her own reflection there now, dimly picked out by the candlelight.

Perhaps that was it, she mused. *Perhaps it was just my reflection, distorted by the cold.*

But Fiona suspected in her hearts of hearts that that wasn't true; that a child's face had appeared to her, staring through the glass.

She stood up and drew the wooden shutters hastily against the night. As she sat on the edge of her bed again, Fiona felt a sudden need to speak to Samuel. She glanced at the clock above her mantelpiece. It was half past ten at night ... too late to be wandering next door to the cottage to wake them up. But she couldn't resist it. She had to.

Throwing her wardrobe door open, she grabbed a jumper and trousers and pulled them on. She crept down the eerie staircase to the floor below. It was so dark. She pressed one or two light switches hopefully but knew they wouldn't respond.

By the time she had arrived in the kitchen, her eyes had adjusted to the gloom, but she was beginning to have second thoughts. What had she really seen out there? And what if it was still lurking outside?

How could a face be floating outside my bedroom window? She shook her head.

I don't care, she thought. *I have to talk to Samuel.*

She took a coat from the peg and pulled on a pair of boots. The heavy outer door squealed on its hinges as she pulled it open.

Although it was cold inside the house, it was even colder outside. There was a silence out on the moor that only snow could bring. Fiona recognized that feeling well. It happened every winter up on Sheriffmuir, and every winter it was quite magical and breathtakingly beautiful.

Tonight, however, it held an eerie possibility.

The fresh fall of snow had eliminated all footprints from the courtyard. No one had walked this way since the families had gone to their respective houses that evening.

She stepped out onto the virgin snow and made her own set of prints to the cottage next door. She didn't go to the kitchen door, as she was afraid to disturb Isabel, but crept instead under the bare plum trees to Samuel's bedroom window in the corner. She stood in the flowerbed and tapped on the glass. No response.

She tried again.

Behind her she heard a noise and spun round quickly, almost stumbling over in her panic.

It was Lucy, one of the dogs, who had followed her outside into the darkness.

"Lucy," she whispered. "You gave me a fright."

She patted the dog on the head and then turned back to the window to try again. She let out a scream loud enough to wake the dead.

The curtains had been pulled back and Samuel's face was staring out at her through the glass. He mouthed words of alarm at her, but she couldn't hear him.

He opened the window with difficulty and tried to push the snow off the ledge so it didn't fall into his room.

"What the ...?"

"What d'you think you're doing, scaring me like that?" Fiona screeched.

"Me? Scaring you?"

She held a hand to her pounding heart. "As if I've not had enough to deal with already," she murmured, half to herself.

He shook his head. "Correct me if I'm wrong, but who is the one tapping on my window in the middle of the night?"

"It's not the middle of the night," she barked. "It's quarter to eleven, actually."

"Oh, well, that's alright then," he said sarcastically. He looked at her and the dog Lucy standing patiently behind her.

"What do you want anyway?"

"To talk to you."

"Well are you going to stand there all night or are you going to come in?"

"Course not. Let me in."

"Come to the back door," he told her, then banged the window shut and disappeared from view.

After a few seconds, the red-painted wooden door clicked open and Fiona was ushered quickly into the kitchen. Lucy followed her hopefully.

"Don't leave dirty prints," Fiona told the dog, urging her to sit beneath the table on the stone flags.

"It's freezing in here," she added, looking about her at the dark kitchen.

"It's freezing everywhere. Now what do you want?"

"Well that's friendly. I told you. I need to talk to you."

"What about?"

They stared at each other in the gloom and Samuel lit a candle on the table.

"What's happened now?" he persisted.

Fiona looked at him, and considered how best to put it. Samuel was watching her closely.

"You've seen something, haven't you?"

Fiona nodded. "I think so, but then again maybe I didn't."

Samuel waited for her to elaborate.

"You won't believe me if I tell you."

"Try me."

"I saw her," Fiona said simply. "Through the window ..."

She glanced at Samuel's face and changed her mind. "It might well have been my own reflection. I suppose ... that's possible, isn't it? But ..."

Samuel nodded thoughtfully. "Of course it's possible. But it wasn't your own reflection, was it?" he said quietly.

She shook her head. "No, I don't think so."

Both of them were silent for a moment, staring at the flame of the candle between them.

"What did she look like?" Samuel asked. "Was she like Charles said?"

"She was young."

"Younger than us?"

"Probably. I'm not sure."

"What was she like?"

Fiona shrugged. "A bit like me, I suppose, only much smaller ... very thin ... and her hair was darker."

They stared at each other for a while, then Samuel continued.

"We need to talk to the others about this in the morning. If your mum gets wind of this ..." Samuel began, "If she even *begins* to suspect that strange things are happening here again, she'll throw a wobbly and threaten to move. You know she will. We have to do something."

Fiona thought about it for a moment. *Were there more ghosts to worry about? More stories left untold?* She shifted in her chair, clicking her fingers for Lucy to come out from under the table.

"I guess it's time I was getting back. We can talk about it properly in the morning."

She glanced towards the closed kitchen door fearfully. She didn't fancy having to go out into the dark again.

Who knew what might be lurking out there? But she was too ashamed to admit that she might be scared.

"D'you want me to come with you?" Samuel offered.

"Don't be daft," Fiona cried, with false heartiness. "What good would that do? You'd only have to come back again ... in your pyjamas," she added. "It's freezing out there."

"You'll be fine," Samuel reassured her.

"Thanks ... that's reassuring," she muttered sarcastically. "Think of me while you're back in your warm bed and I'm facing who knows what outside!"

"You've got Lucy with you," he protested. She grunted.

"S'pose so. See you later."

Samuel stood on the doorstep and watched Fiona walk across the courtyard towards the big house. "Bye then," he called out, partly to encourage her. "See you in the morning."

She turned and waved, before vanishing beneath the archway, towards her own house.

The cold crept around his feet and he shivered inside his slippers and dressing gown. He waited a moment or two, listening to the silence, then closed the door of the cottage.

A while later, Fiona had almost succeeded in falling asleep, when Lucy suddenly stood up. Fiona heard her claws clicking against the wooden floorboards. The dog stood near the half-open door, ears flattened, body tense and began to release a low threatening growl.

"What is it, Lucy? What is it, girl?"

But the dog remained where she was, refusing to budge.

Fiona crept out of bed, taking a few tentative steps towards the door, her heart pounding.

The dog never moved from her position.

Fiona knew that the corridor outside would be pitch-black. She'd be able to see nothing.

Fearfully, she put her hand on the door knob, and pulled the door open a fraction, her heart hammering in her chest like a drum.

A light was glimmering in the dark deserted corridor.

Fiona stared.

The girl stared back, a candle held high in one hand.

"Hello!"

Her face was pale and gleaming.

Fiona screamed, slammed the door shut and ran back to her bed. She stayed there, shivering, watching the pool of light under the crack of the door. Lucy had started to bark.

Suddenly there was a flurry of footsteps and the

light vanished abruptly. The door burst open and Chris Morton appeared, looking ruffled and dishevelled.

"What is it?"

"Mum," Fiona cried, clutching at her mother in a way she hadn't done for years.

"What on earth is it? A nightmare?"

"Yes, yes, that was it."

Despite her terror, Fiona was even more determined to keep quiet about what she'd just seen. She made a huge effort to pull herself together.

She'd talk to the others in the morning, maybe, but they mustn't let their mother know what was happening ... otherwise she'd sell up and leave. And they couldn't let that happen.

"I'm fine, Mum. It was just a silly nightmare. It must have been that cheese sandwich I had before bed. They're supposed to give you weird dreams. I guess I gave Lucy a fright too."

Chris Morton shook her head. "D'you want Lucy to stay in here for the night?"

"I don't mind," Fiona murmured, trying to play it down.

"Well, if you're sure ..."

"I'm fine now, honestly."

"Go to sleep then," Chris Morton instructed her and closed the bedroom door behind her.

All was quiet in the house. A little girl with ice-cold hands paused at the head of the staircase and peered down. She had been bored for many a long year, but now life was just beginning to get interesting again.

Outside it was snowing. She remembered how that used to look, when the trees were glittering and leaning under the weight of it. Everything would turn to glass as it slowly froze under the blue light of the moon. Winters were so much colder back then.

She heard someone approaching on the staircase. Chris Morton was climbing the stairs back to her room, after fetching a hot drink from the kitchen.

The little girl leant over the banister and watched in silence.

Chris Morton pressed a light switch and the first-floor landing glowed with artificial light. The little girl melted away. The older woman was talking to herself, while the girl listened, invisible as air.

"Thank goodness. The power's back on."

The upstairs corridor was bathed in light. This annoyed the little girl. She preferred the shadows. She lifted her nightrobe and swept in silence.

The electric lights were evenly spaced along the walls, brown glass globes that each gave off a soft light. The light switch controlled all six of them; they were not independent of each other.

On impulse she decided to play a little game. As Chris Morton walked along the upstairs corridor, Eliza made the lights go out behind her ... one by one. Chris Morton turned and stared. She was a brave woman: she was unafraid of the dark, or of loneliness, otherwise she would not have lived here, in so isolated a place.

The lights continued to go out behind her, until at last she was left in total darkness, with the light switch nowhere in reach. She glanced behind her. The corridor was one long tunnel of darkness. Her rational side told her that the wiring in this house was decidedly peculiar and needed looking at ... but her imagination could feel a presence at the end of the corridor ... someone watching her. *Don't be ridiculous,* she told herself. *There's no one there. Just another power cut.*

Chris Morton appeared in her daughter's room.

"Fiona," she whispered hoarsely.

No answer.

Something stirred under the duvet in the four-poster bed.

Fiona sat up, looking puzzled.

"Mum? Is that you?"

"Just checking to see if you're still awake," Chris murmured, somewhat breathlessly.

"Well, I was asleep, but ..."

"I've brought you a hot drink. The electricity came back on for a moment and then went off in a rather strange way." She told Fiona what had happened. "Must be the wiring," she finished. "I keep meaning to get it checked. Anyway ..." She placed a steaming mug on the bedside table and patted her daughter's arm. "Night then."

"Night."

Reluctantly Chris Morton closed the door behind her and ventured out onto the dark landing. She returned to her own room telling herself that nothing out of the ordinary had happened.

The Other Side

The next morning the children got together to discuss Fiona's nocturnal sighting of Eliza, and what it meant.

"I knew there was something wrong with Lucy," Fiona explained to the others. "She just wouldn't settle. Then I saw this light under the door, in the corridor outside. I opened it and there she was ... just standing looking at me, with a lighted candle in her hand. That's when I screamed and Mum came."

"D'you think she suspects anything?"

"Mum, you mean? I don't think so," Fiona said. "I told her it was a bad dream ... but she's not stupid. She might put two and two together."

"It's very important that we don't let on about Eliza and all this other weird stuff that's been happening," Charles told the others. "We don't want Mum freaking out and deciding that it's time to move."

"She'd never move, surely?" Samuel cried. "You've been here too long ... your family, I mean."

Charles and Sebastian looked doubtful. "She has bad memories about the place, though. She didn't move here until she got married. She might be glad of an excuse to leave," Sebastian murmured.

"We can't let that happen," Fiona cut in.

"At least the power's back on," Samuel said, flicking a light switch on and off, just for the pleasure of it.

"I hope our days here aren't numbered," Charles added forlornly.

"Are you kidding?" Sebastian said. "Dodgy wiring, secret staircases, mouldy passageways, ghosts in the walls ... who'd want to stay?"

"We do," Charles and Fiona said at the same time, without meaning to.

On the other side, the ghost girl drifted ... free at last. She left her brother behind in the dismal room, crying his heart out, crying for the past ... and for their mother.

There was no point in doing that, Eliza knew. Their destiny, their future, lay with the children who had found the secret staircase.

She sailed through the air, passing through walls and panelling as easily as water flowing through a pipe. The boy Charles's bedroom was empty. There was no one there this time. *Oh well*, she thought, and drifted on.

She liked the freedom, but longed for some solidity to her body. She was having some fun now, discovering what she was capable of. She hadn't meant to smash things in Isabel's studio; she had had a fright on realizing that she had strayed from the house unwittingly and had been in a rush to get back. But the vase had been deliberate ... and highly successful in making her presence felt.

She hadn't meant to scare anyone. She had just wanted to see what she could do with the lights. But tonight she seemed to have succeeded in scaring both Fiona and her mother.

The passing of time was nothing to Eliza; it either went very quickly, like a speed train passing through a tunnel, or so slowly that nothing at all seemed to move, and even the journey of one tiny mouse across a carpet could turn into a mammoth adventure, lasting for what appeared to be days. As the sun rose above the snowy moor, casting a reddish glow over everything, Eliza barely noticed the breaking of day. She was travelling through the house, on an expedition of her own.

The grandfather clock chimed in the empty hallway, striking away the hours. Eliza recognized some of the paintings on the wall from her own lifetime. She sometimes heard faint echoes from a past that no living being could possibly hear.

Her little brother was too afraid to accompany her. He didn't like to be on the other side. He preferred to remain in the shadows, trapped in time. But Eliza wanted more than that. They had woken from their slumber, after four hundred years of restless sleeping. Only once before had they been woken from their slumber, when Catherine Morton had slept in the tower as a child. She used to hear them sometimes, through the walls. But they had never before managed to drift to the other side. Until now.

Now that Eliza had spoken with the boy Charles, she felt sure that things would be different.

Despite the snow, Granny and Mr Hughes had still managed to get home each night and back to Dunadd the next day, although they had nearly given up this morning, as the roads were getting increasingly worse. Not much defeated Granny, however, not even the wildest snowstorm or severest blizzard.

A cruel light glimmered on the moor outside. It was freezing, turning pockets of land blue and transforming the branches into ice features. Eliza floated, shivering. "So beautiful," she murmured to herself, gazing out at the purest white landscape. "So beautiful."

Downstairs, she hovered in the hallway, hanging back in the shadows. She could hear voices coming from the direction of the kitchen. Fiona was discussing something with her mother and the old woman, Granny Hughes. Something about a pet rabbit.

Eliza watched, her sad dark eyes gleaming.

That girl has a mother, Eliza thought. *A mother who cares for her and worries about her. And what have we?* It had been so long since Eliza had known what real life was like. Her thoughts became too painful. She did not like to think about her own mother.

A floorboard creaked and three pairs of eyes turned to the open kitchen doorway.

"What was that?" Chris Morton said.

Fiona peered into the gloom of the hallway.

Behind her Granny muttered, "Your mum told me about your secret staircase."

"What?" She turned her attention back to the kitchen and the adults waiting there.

"Secret passageways and the like," Granny was murmuring, as she busied herself at the sink. "You'll never get me cleaning in that library again, knowing what I now know, you mark my words."

"But you didn't use to clean it before," Fiona said. "Remember? You said it gave you the creeps."

"Aye, that's right. And now it gives me the creeps a hundredfold worse."

Fiona laughed. "A hundredfold? What kind of word is that?"

Mrs Morton laughed softly, listening to this exchange.

Granny sniffed. "Don't they teach you to use a dictionary at that fancy school of yours, then? Mind you don't go poking about any more, with that friend of yours. There's enough trouble at the moment ... what with the lights going on and off and the power being so unpredictable and all, without you adding to it."

"How would we add to it?"

"Creeping about," she barked.

"I don't creep."

"Yes you do, young lady ... you creep," Granny barked crossly. "That's how you discover things you're not supposed to ... like that secret passageway, for instance. It's not healthy, so it isn't."

"Now, now Granny, don't take on so," Mrs Morton interrupted, trying to keep the peace. Granny scrubbed at a pan with more ferocity than the task strictly warranted.

"It comes from reading too many books. Too much thinking never did nobody any good." She slammed the pan down on the draining board. "And that's a fact."

Ignoring her, Fiona went back to the doorway and looked out.

Eliza pressed herself flat, almost merging with the grandfather cock. No one saw her, but Fiona wandered out into the hall and stared hard into the shadows, right at the spot where Eliza was hiding.

Fiona realized at once that the substance of the air around her had changed subtly. She pulled the kitchen door closed behind her so that the adults were cut off. Then she turned to face the darkness.

Like the night before, her fingers and toes alerted her immediately to the extreme cold of Eliza's presence.

She could see the ghost girl now, staring at her, eyes wide and gleaming. There was something hungry about their expression.

Eliza spoke. "Hello."

Fiona jumped back in alarm. With one nervous hand, she reached out to see what she felt like. But she stopped before she got there and recoiled. There was a chalky substance all over her, caked on in places, like flour.

"Was it you I saw? Last night ... outside my window?" Fiona asked.

The ghost girl was silent.

"Why were you looking in?"

Eliza blinked her large eyes soulfully. "I didst not

intend to scare you," she said. "I just wanted to see your room."

"Who are you?" Fiona whispered, glancing nervously over her shoulder to make sure the door to the kitchen was still firmly shut, and that the adults couldn't hear.

"I have already spoken my name, to your brother, I believe. I am Eliza Morton."

Fiona stared.

"I'm Fiona," she stuttered.

"Fiona," the girl repeated softly.

"Can I ask you a question?" Fiona asked. The girl nodded her assent. Fiona continued. "What year is it?"

"Why, it is the year of Our Lord, 1604," she replied, her voice as clear as a bell. Then she giggled. An eerie chuckle that unsettled Fiona. She was instantly aware of how cold the hallway had become. An icy breeze seemed to be seeping in under the floorboards. She glanced at the window at the end of the hallway, at the bottom of the stairs. It was a deep-set picturesque window, with several panes of glass. Snow was drifting down past the tower, big fluffy flakes swirling endlessly in the air.

Eliza followed her gaze and let out a small exclamation. "Ah. It is snowing."

"How old are you?" Fiona persisted.

"I am nine years of age."

"Only nine?"

"So I believe," Eliza replied, her voice prim and proper as she carefully enunciated her words in her formal language. It sounded strange on Fiona's ears, distant, yet oddly romantic.

"My brother and I were sleeping. But you woke us."

"How did we wake you?"

Eliza shrugged. "You started talking about us. You saw us in the tapestry and then you tapped on our wall. You found our secret passageway. And your brother wrote a ghost story. Or made an attempt to. It was good enough to find us."

She giggled again.

"Can I ask you another question?" Fiona said. "Whose house is this?"

"Why, it is my father's, of course. But he is no longer here," she finished sadly.

"Where has he gone?" Fiona asked.

Eliza put her head on one side, quizzically, and appeared to be perplexed. "I know not!"

"And your mother?" Fiona added.

Suddenly Eliza's face was transformed. Her eyes gleamed with pent-up fury.

"I have no mother."

"Surely," Fiona murmured. "Surely you must have a mother. Everyone does."

"Not I."

"Why not?"

Eliza stared hard at Fiona, her eyes suddenly desperately sad.

Then she whispered in a small voice "She left us to die."

At that moment the kitchen door burst open and Granny appeared, grappling with the Hoover. Fiona glanced back over her shoulder.

"Blast this wretched thing," Granny was muttering under her breath.

When Fiona turned back, the girl had gone. Vanished into thin air before either of the two adults could see her. But not before Fiona had had time to ask her some essential questions. She felt as if she was getting somewhere, at last. She had to tell the others.

She found the boys upstairs, gathered in the drawing room. Samuel could instantly tell from her expression that something was wrong.

"What is it?" he asked.

"I saw her," Fiona burst out. "I saw Eliza. I spoke to her this time. She told me what they're doing here. She said ..." but then Fiona hesitated. She wondered exactly what Eliza had told her, wondered what to make of it exactly. It was all a bit muddled. "... she said it was 1604."

The boys stared at her, uncomprehending.

"That's what she said," Fiona insisted. "She said ... it was the year of Our Lord, 1604."

"She's stuck in time," Charles said. "In her own time."

"But she can see us," Fiona finished.

"Where does that leave us?" Sebastian said.

"It leaves us with a very confused and troubled ghost girl. Two troubled ghost children," Fiona added, "who feel as if they've been abandoned by their mother."

"How do you know that?" Samuel asked.

Fiona's brow wrinkled and she looked pensive and sad for a moment. "It was something she said, that's all."

"What?" Samuel was insistent.

Fiona hesitated a moment. "She said ... she said that their mother had left them to die."

All four children fell silent, allowing the facts to digest.

"How horrible," Samuel murmured.

"Isn't it?" Fiona said.

"What did she mean?" Charles added. "Their mother left them to die? How? What happened?"

"Now that," Fiona sighed, "we don't know. Not yet anyway."

"How do we find out?" Sebastian said.

"I know," Samuel put in quickly, catching Fiona's

eye. "There's an old friend we haven't visited in a while."

"Mr MacFarlane," Fiona muttered.

"He might know something," Samuel said. "He knows lots about the history of Sheriffmuir. And maybe there's another family ghost story that he hasn't told you about."

Charles was sceptical. "But he can't know every-thing."

Fiona rolled her eyes. "You're only fourteen so you definitely don't know everything. But Mr MacFarlane's ... well, he's ..."

"Old?" Samuel supplied the word.

"Exactly. He's ancient."

"He's not *that* ancient," Sebastian put in. "He's fit enough to look after himself, anyway."

"I suppose it's worth a try," Charles admitted finally.

Their voices faded away into silence.

A child sat alone in the darkness. No one knew he was there. On the floor before him was a group of clumsy-looking toy soldiers, roughly carved from wood. The red paint on them was faded and peeling, but the boy didn't notice. He moved them around, dragging them through the dirt, pretending to march them across an imaginary battlefield. It was a way of keeping his misery at bay. He was pretending, entering a world of make-believe, where his only comfort was to be found.

They were primitive-looking toys, scarred and marked by their great age. The boy's loving hands had worn them smooth with handling. They were all he had: the only souvenirs from a life long since faded away. Everything the boy had once known had crumbled into disrepair, leaving nothing but this forlorn little corner of the building, where he and his sister had slept for so many hundreds of years, like children in a fairy tale, waiting to be woken. And now that they were awake ... what now? Were they to be forever haunted by their own dreadful memories?

He let go of his toy soldiers so that they fell, unsupported, to the ground. Even the world of make-believe could let us down, sometimes.

Eliza found her brother in the dusty room they inhabited together. He was still crying. With a rare touch of compassion, Eliza put her arm around him.

"Cease that noise. I have returned."

"But you will leave me again," he whispered. "I know you will."

Lynns Farm

"I really don't see how he can help," Sebastian was saying, as they crunched their way through the deepening snow towards the waterfall.

"He was helpful last time," Fiona reminded the others.

"I don't think he'll take kindly to us just turning up, though," Charles said uneasily. "It's only you and Samuel he knows properly."

"He won't mind," Fiona reassured her brother. "Anyway, it's always good to see Mr MacFarlane. Granny Hughes said we should check up on him in this weather. Make sure he's alright. We'll be doing a neighbourly turn."

Her brothers followed her and Samuel past the waterfall, through the trees to the lonely little farmhouse set in its isolated grounds. The sunlight rarely penetrated this low-lying piece of ground where Lynns Farmhouse stood, sheltered on all sides by trees and high ridges of land.

Patrick MacFarlane lived here alone, with his dog

and his memories. He was not an unhappy man, despite his solitude and eccentricity, and he'd been delighted by Samuel and Fiona's attempts to make friends with him. It had opened up a little window in his lonely life. They didn't visit him often, but when they did, he always found it entertaining.

He was not expecting them, however, and they had no way of knowing if he was actually in. They approached the door nervously, peering at the windows to see if there was any life behind them.

"Mr MacFarlane!" Samuel knocked on the door and called out his name.

Silence. An eerie uncomfortable silence. They couldn't even hear the dog barking. A blanket of disappointment drifted down like the snow and landed on their shoulders. It was unsettling.

"Oh," Samuel said. "Where would he be in this weather?"

"See?" Charles snapped tetchily. "I told you."

"*What* did you tell us?" Fiona replied.

"That there was no point. That he wouldn't be in!"

"No you didn't," Samuel corrected him. "You just said you didn't want to bother, that was all."

"I did not," he cried, rounding on Samuel.

"Ach, for goodness sake!" A voice broke in. "Stop that bickering. I can hear you a mile off."

They turned to see Patrick MacFarlane making his way towards them through the snow, his arms full of chopped firewood, the dog at his heels.

Fiona's face lit up. "How are you Mr MacFarlane?" she beamed.

"Och, I'm not so bad. And yourselves?"

"We're good," Samuel said.

"I see you've brought your big brothers this time?" he observed, looking at Charles and Sebastian keenly.

"That's right," Fiona said.

"So ... what brings you to my door?"

"Questions ..." she blurted out, looking at him desperately. "We were wondering if you knew any stories about other ghosts up at the house?"

He looked at her shrewdly. "More research?"

"That's right," Fiona said.

"And what kind of ghosts would these be?"

"Two children," she said. "A brother and sister. Very young. The girl is about nine, we think."

"Two children?" He looked perplexed and shook his head.

"From 1604?" Fiona added hopefully.

"Now ... that doesn't ring any bells, I'm afraid. Not this time, it doesn't."

The children's hearts sank in disappointment. They had been hoping he would be able to point them immediately in the right direction. He always seemed so knowledgeable about the history of Sheriffmuir. They had hoped that maybe they could glean another tiny piece of information from him: a missing piece of the jigsaw which would help to solve the riddle of the mystery children.

"Well, come in anyway," he commanded, "out of the cold."

They followed him into the kitchen, which was rather dusty, but comfortable all the same. There were books and magazines piled up on chairs. An open fire dominated the room, with a large old-fashioned hearth that had been an original feature of the house when it was first built four hundred years ago. Little had changed since, in many ways. The house had not really been modernized since the fifties, so much of it was in need of attention, but Patrick MacFarlane liked it exactly the way it was and so did Samuel and Fiona.

"So," he said, dropping the logs into a basket next to the fireplace and bending down to light a match. The kindling took immediately and a bright fire blazed up the chimney.

Patrick MacFarlane leant on the wide wooden mantelpiece with his elbow and regarded his guests for a moment.

"What's bin happening up at Dunadd then?"

Fiona gave a huge sigh. "Where do I begin?"

"Oh, it's like that, is it?" Mr MacFarlane said. "You'd better have a seat then. And you two boys as well," he added, glancing at Charles and Sebastian, who were lurking in the background, looking rather awkward.

Chair legs scraped against the tiles as they made themselves comfortable.

"1604 you said?" Mr MacFarlane pondered, regarding Fiona thoughtfully. "I know I'm ancient, but my memory doesn't stretch that far back, I'm afraid. And why that year precisely?"

The children looked at each other warily.

"Because it's what she said," Fiona admitted.

"Who?" Mr MacFarlane said, piercingly, his eyes on Fiona.

"The ghost girl ... child spirit ... whatever you want to call her."

"She spoke to you?"

Fiona nodded. "And to Charles as well."

"Really?" Mr MacFarlane looked at her older brother for confirmation. Charles nodded.

"What did she say?" the old man asked, trying to stifle his alarm.

"She said her name's Eliza," Fiona burst out. "When I asked her what year it was, she said it was 1604. She claims that we've woken her and her brother."

"It was my fault really," Samuel cut in. "Because it was me who found the secret staircase in the library."

"A secret staircase?" Mr MacFarlane repeated, his amazement showing on his face.

"That's right. Behind the fireplace."

"I didn't know about that," he said quietly.

"Neither did we," Fiona added. "Mum didn't either."

"So your mother knows about this then?" Mr MacFarlane sighed.

Fiona nodded.

"And what did she have to say about it?"

"Nothing much, really," Fiona began.

The old man raised his eyebrows and looked at her in disbelief.

"Well ..." Fiona qualified her meaning "... she thought it might be a priest hole or something like that, even though there was no little room or cubby-hole behind the fireplace. Just the staircase and the passageway beyond it."

"We didn't tell her about the noises we'd heard ... nor about the ghost girl," Samuel added.

"Why not?" Mr MacFarlane asked, although he could guess their reasons.

"We don't want her getting any ideas about moving," Fiona cried. "You have to understand ... we don't want to move house. We want to stay put."

"And you think she might entertain the idea if she knew what else has been happening?"

"That's right." Fiona hung her head, staring at her feet.

"You could be right," he muttered softly, almost to himself. "Eliza, you said her name was?"

All four children nodded vigorously. "I don't know anything about an Eliza," Mr MacFarlane muttered quietly, almost to himself.

"She and her brother have been in the house all this time," Fiona said.

"And you have no idea what they're doing there, or why they've suddenly appeared?"

"Not really," Fiona murmured.

"I think she's angry," Samuel added. "She broke things, in my mum's studio ..."

"We don't know that for sure," Fiona cut in.

"And we think she smashed a vase in the house."

Fiona looked thoughtful for a moment. "She said their mother had left them to die."

She disliked saying the words out loud. They sounded so bleak and dismal, put bluntly like that.

"Poor children," Mr MacFarlane muttered under his breath. "But there must be more to it than that."

"That's what I thought," Fiona cried, relief flooding her face. "I thought it can't really be as bad as all that.

No mother would do that to her own children, would she? Surely?"

No one seemed to want to answer that question.

"And what made you think of coming to speak to me about it?" Mr MacFarlane said quietly.

"Well, you know so much about the surrounding history of the place," Fiona explained, as if that much was obvious. "You've lived on Sheriffmuir all your life."

"So I have," he murmured, "but I can't tell you anything about a ghost girl and her brother."

The children looked badly disappointed. "We could look it up though," he added. "We've got a date to be going on with, anyway."

"Do you have any books?" Sebastian asked, hopefully, then realizing what a silly question it was, he grew quiet again.

"Aye, I have one or two," Mr MacFarlane said sagely. "Do you?"

Sebastian lowered his head sheepishly.

"Anyway," he grunted, as he eased himself up from his chair. "Hot chocolate anybody? Come on, now. It's snowing out there. You'll be needing something warm inside yer bellies."

"That'd be great, thanks," Fiona replied for them all. She'd inadvertently become the elected spokesperson, seeing as her brothers had become so tongue-tied in the old man's presence.

Mr MacFarlane moved towards the Aga and began pouring milk into a heavy iron saucepan.

"You can go through into the sitting room, if you like, and look at the bookshelves. You might find one or two there about local history. Flick to the index and see if you can find anything pertaining to the date you mention. 16 ... what was it again?"

"1604," Fiona supplied helpfully.

"That's the one."

Charles and Sebastian got up, glad of an opportunity to leave the room and could be heard rummaging in the room next door.

"Second shelf down. On the left," Mr MacFarlane shouted instructions through to them.

"Don't know if they'll come up with anything," he added, "but it'll keep them busy, nonetheless."

"How's that mother of yours?" he added then, glancing in Fiona's direction as he poured a stream of frothy hot chocolate into cups. "Still quibbling about that field of mine?"

Fiona blushed. It had been a bone of contention between Patrick MacFarlane and her mother: some argument over a disputed piece of land. Fiona's mother had claimed it belonged to the Dunadd estate and Mr MacFarlane had been unable to take the case to court, so he'd had to back down in the end as he couldn't afford to pay the solicitor's fees, and decided it wasn't worth the trouble. That was all Fiona knew about the matter. However, it had been enough to sour relations between the two adults. "And neighbours an' all," Granny had snorted contemptuously, in her own inimitable way.

"Well," he said. "What do you think this Eliza Morton wants?"

It was the obvious question and one which had been exercising Samuel and Fiona's minds all day.

"I don't know," Fiona said, running her hand thoughtfully over the knotted grain of the old table.

"It could be anything," Samuel said. "It could be revenge."

"Or a desire for peace," Mr MacFarlane pointed out.

"Or she might want to be free," Fiona said.

"Or ... she could just be having a bit of fun," Samuel added.

"A mischief-maker?" Mr MacFarlane looked impressed. "That's a possibility."

It was at this point that the boys came through from the other room, clutching a book.

Charles laid it on the table and flicked through the pages. "It's got a section on the history of Sheriffmuir," he said, bending his head low over the page. "It mentions the battle, of course. But there's nothing about 1604, or anything round about that time."

"I wonder how they died?" he speculated, becoming more talkative now as he picked up his cup of hot chocolate and began to sip it.

"D'you think they were murdered?" Sebastian blurted out suddenly, his face draining of colour. "In some gruesome and grisly way."

Mr MacFarlane looked reproving. "That's enough speculation. It doesn't help."

"I feel so sorry for them," Fiona murmured.

Charles was quiet. "Me too." His voice was so low they barely heard it.

"We haven't seen the boy, only Eliza, but we've heard them talking. He seems like a very frightened little boy," Fiona explained.

"I wonder what happened to them?" Samuel said.

"Well, maybe something up at the house will tell you more?" Mr MacFarlane pointed out. "Remember ... that library of yours is packed with information."

The children nodded.

"I only wish I could have been more help," he added.

They drank their hot chocolate in silence now.

The room was dark apart from the firelight, although it was still early afternoon. Samuel glanced towards the window and noticed that it was snowing more heavily.

"You'd better watch out for that weather," Mr MacFarlane commented, following Samuel's gaze. He threw another log onto the fire so that sparks flew up the chimney. "We don't want you getting lost in that snow now, do we?"

Sleepover

Mr MacFarlane had given them plenty to think about as they trudged their way home. It was an ordeal trying to labour up a steep hill through the deepening snow. It was falling more heavily now as the sky began to scowl ominously, and they were very weary as they managed the last part of their journey. The trees formed a white tunnel overhead as they approached the house.

They could hear the dogs barking.

"Only us," Fiona called, as she threw her boots off in the passageway, making a fuss of Lucy, her favourite.

"Where've you all been?" Chris Morton asked.

"Nowhere," Fiona replied guiltily.

"Just out for a walk," Charles said.

"In this weather?"

He shrugged and nodded.

"It's not like you four to stick so closely together. Still, if it means you're getting along, suits me fine."

They all knew they weren't really supposed to visit

Lynns Farmhouse. Their mother wasn't keen on Mr MacFarlane and still bore a grudge about their recent dispute. Granny Hughes thought the whole thing was absurd and had said as much.

"Is my mum here at all?" Samuel asked now.

"She's in her studio I think," Mrs Morton told him.

"Where else?" he sighed.

"She's doing rather well, I gather. Has one or two commissions lined up."

Granny rolled her eyes. "Just so long as they pay," she snorted under her breath.

"You can have some supper here, if you like?" Mrs Morton offered. Samuel looked hopefully towards the oven. His mother wasn't the best of cooks and the idea of eating something prepared by Granny Hughes – usually a casserole of some sort – was rather appealing, especially after walking through the snow.

"Thanks," he said. "It's freezing outside."

"Something hot will do you good. Actually," she added, "nip across to the studio and ask your mum if she'd like something. Save her cooking. We can always send it out to her, like relief workers, if she doesn't want to stop chiselling or whatever she's doing." Chris Morton laughed to herself quietly.

Granny meanwhile was preparing to leave Sheriffmuir for the night. She pulled on her woollen headscarf and knotted it severely under her chin. Her husband hovered nearby, jangling the car keys in his hand.

"Are you sure you'll be alright," Mrs Morton asked them anxiously. "You know you can stay here for the night."

"Ach, no," Granny sniffed. "I'd rather not. I like to get home."

Mr Hughes sighed. "We'll be fine, so we will."

As they drove away, Charles looked out of the window. The snow had been falling relentlessly all day, smothering the moor. It had probably gathered in unexpected places, in the hollows and dips, waiting to take the wary traveller by surprise.

"They won't get far," he predicted.

"Look on the bright side, why don't you!" Sebastian quipped.

"Granny's so stubborn," Fiona said. "She'll make it somehow."

As they sat down to eat at the kitchen table, the snow was still coming down, building up on the window ledges and gathering in the corners of the glass panes.

"It would actually be really pretty if it didn't mean we will probably be stuck here," Fiona said.

"I quite like it," Samuel added, spearing a piece of meat onto his fork.

"Even the solitude?"

He nodded. "It's atmospheric."

Suddenly the lights flickered. "Uh-oh," Mrs Morton said. "Here we go again."

A buzz could be heard fizzing overhead, then there was a loud bang from the basement, as if something had short-circuited. The rooms were plunged into sudden darkness.

Chris Morton sighed. "Looks like the circuit board has fused again ... but quite spectacularly this time. Or else the snow's brought the power lines down." She reached behind to the dresser for a clutch of candles and tea-lights. "Must be the weather," she remarked. "If it wasn't for you and your mother, Samuel, I don't know how we'd manage up here from one day to the next. We'd never see a living soul at this time of year."

Fiona began lighting tea-lights and the kitchen soon glimmered into life.

"It's rather romantic actually," Mrs Morton said cheerfully, examining the table in front of her.

"I wonder how long it will be off for this time?" Fiona asked.

"Perhaps I should call somebody? Get it checked." Her mother was speaking to herself now.

"One of us could try the electrics," Charles suggested. "See if a fuse has blown."

But his mother wasn't sure she liked that idea. She left the others eating at the table and went to the hall telephone, returning a few minutes later.

"That's odd."

"What is?" asked Sebastian.

"Telephone's down as well. Go across to your cottage when you've eaten, Samuel, and see if yours is working, would you?"

"Try your mobile," Fiona suggested. "See if you can get a signal."

"In this weather?"

Mrs Morton wandered into the corridor with her mobile phone clamped to her ear.

"Nope. No signal. I'll try again later. Not to worry. We've got candles and open fires. We should be okay for a while. It won't last long," she said confidently, more for her own benefit than anyone else's.

Down in the glen where the narrow road crossed over the Wharry Burn, Granny and Mr Hughes had not got far. They were stuck. They stood forlornly next to their little car, gazing at it. The snow had drifted and it was impossible to get through.

"Ach, well," Mr Hughes muttered. "Thought that'd be the case, so I did. We'll just have to walk back to the house, I suppose." He sounded resolved.

He put his arm round his wife. "Come on, now. It's not far."

Granny looked up at the house through the trees. It didn't look very welcoming.

"Lights have all gone out," she observed, in a gloomy voice.

"So they have," Mr Hughes confirmed.

They trudged their way slowly back to Dunadd, beneath the tunnel of white trees. The bleak house stared back at them balefully, its windows blank. Granny Hughes shivered, pulling her headscarf a little tighter.

Everyone was relieved when Granny and her husband reappeared through the snow.

"I'm glad you came back," Chris Morton admitted. "We were worried about you. Besides, we now have a little problem," and she glanced in Mr Hughes's direction. "How are you with electrics, Jim?"

"Ach, well ..." he began, unconvincingly.

Although they looked to see if a fuse had blown, there was nothing obvious, so they promptly gave up.

"We'll just have to wait till morning," Chris said.

Later that night, with no power, no electricity and no heat – apart from the open fires – the adults decided on a sleepover for the children.

"They can sleep next to the fire in the drawing room," Mrs Morton suggested to Isabel. "With plenty of pillows and sleeping bags. That should do the trick."

Isabel readily agreed. "At least they'll stay warm that way."

They banked the fire up until it was roaring. Outside the trees could only be seen dimly through a gentle curtain of white snowflakes, but the huge drawing room flickered with orange and crimson light from the big stone fireplace.

"I'll leave you lot to sleep then. No wandering about in the night, okay?" Chris Morton instructed them.

They nodded their heads obediently and prepared to snuggle down, lying as close to the flames as they dared without scorching their feet. The hearth was so wide it could take plenty of large logs.

"This is fantastic," Samuel said, wriggling his toes contentedly.

Charles leaned his back against a sofa, reading a book by the light of a single candle, snug inside his sleeping bag.

"You'll hurt your eyes like that," Fiona commented.

He ignored her.

As the house fell silent around them, the adults having retreated to their beds, Samuel leaned towards the others.

"Hey," he whispered, "we can use this as an excellent opportunity to do some more research."

"Great idea," Fiona agreed.

Sebastian looked less enthusiastic. "Ghost hunting again? The whole house is in darkness," he pointed out.

"Exactly," Samuel said. "The perfect conditions. No one will see us."

"Apart from *you-know-who!*" Fiona shuddered slightly.

"What does she look like, anyway?" Samuel asked his friend, suddenly gripped by a morbid curiosity.

"Charles will tell you. Kind of thin and hungry-looking," Fiona murmured quietly.

Charles looked up from his book. "She had sad eyes. There were shadows under them ... and this white powdery stuff on her clothes and hair and things."

"What d'you mean?" Samuel asked.

"I don't know," Charles said. "I can't explain it."

Samuel thought for a moment.

"I think we should look in the library, for books ... for anything that might have some information ... like Mr Macfarlane said."

"On you go then," Charles said.

Samuel stood up and went next door to explore the bookshelves. Fiona followed him, but soon decided against it.

"It's too cold away from the fire," she complained and ran back to the warmth.

Samuel selected one or two books with promising titles – *Disappearing Communities of Sheriffmuir* and *Sheriffmuir: A Brief History* – and brought them back with him. He plonked them on the floor next to his sleeping bag. By the light of the flames, he opened their hard leather covers and turned the pages. "Maybe one of these will tell us something about what was going on in 1604," Samuel muttered. "Historically, I mean."

"That doesn't mean to say it will explain what happened to Eliza and her brother," Fiona pointed out.

"Or how they were murdered," Sebastian added.

She rounded on her brother sharply. "We don't know that they *were* murdered."

"Just a wild guess!"

Samuel peered closely at the text in front of him.

"What is it?" Fiona leant over his shoulder.

"It says in this one, *Disappearing Communities of Sheriffmuir*, by H.R. Black, that there was an outbreak of plague in this area in 1600 ... in the surrounding villages of the foothills. There's no mention of Sheriffmuir, though, or Dunadd. Hang on ... there's more."

Samuel read the passage out loud, while the others listened.

"There were occasional outbreaks of plague in the area, although exact dates are largely confused and do not always correspond. It wasn't unknown for the victims to be buried in separate graveyards, set apart especially for the purpose: plague graveyards, which are easily discernible today owing to the headstones' markings of a skull and crossbones to denote the cause of death. However, it was not uncommon for the victims to be disposed of unceremoniously in mass graves rather than private graves. Their bodies would have been slung in sacks and covered in lime, to avoid contamination and the spread of disease, although whether the method worked or not is a moot point. These plague pits would have been covered with earth and left unmarked. Today, it is difficult to ascertain the exact location and whereabouts of these places, although it is likely they would lie outside, or on the outskirts, of any built-up areas such as towns, villages or cities."

"What does 'moot' mean?" Sebastian glanced at the others.

Samuel shrugged.

"It's a phrase," Charles said. "It means they don't really know if it worked or not."

"Well, there's no point worrying about it now anyway," Fiona added.

"Young children died all the time back then," Charles said. "What did they call it? Infant mortality?"

"Perhaps that was it," Fiona murmured. "The plague would explain it."

"But why blame their mother for what happened? No, I don't think it's that," Samuel said.

It was getting late and far too chilly to move away from the warmth of the fireplace. They gradually nodded off, one by one. Charles was secretly relieved about not having to sleep in his own room that night, after his recent experiences. It wasn't that he was particularly frightened, he told himself, it was just that … what with the loss of power and everything … it was good to have some company. Usually such a loner, he was enjoying the unaccustomed camaraderie.

As the four children lay sleeping, one candle remained lit. Without warning it suddenly flickered and went out. A dim shape appeared in the far corner of the room.

Fiona, Samuel, Charles and Sebastian lay still. No one moved, as the child spirit crept closer. She stared down at them, individually, observing them. Samuel twitched slightly in his sleep, as he felt a chill shadow pass across his face. But he didn't wake.

Eliza looked thin and cold, shivering in her inadequate shift. She drifted over the children, then moved towards the library. She was having fun, exploring the house in the dark. She was relearning all the old places she used to visit as a child, when she was a living, breathing human individual, with a mother and a father and a future before her.

The firelight threw moving shapes against the far walls and into the distant corners of the room. Suddenly Eliza paused. One of the children by the fireplace had sat up and was rubbing his eyes.

She stared at him.

He stared back.

It was Samuel.

She stood frozen for a moment, then lifted a hand and beckoned him with one finger.

He hesitated and considered waking the others. But Eliza didn't seem to want that.

She urged him to follow her.

So he did.

He got up out of his sleeping bag, paused for a moment to glance at Fiona and the boys, then followed Eliza out of the drawing room onto the landing outside.

Samuel stared at the apparition before him. He had never seen her before, knowing of her only through Fiona and Charles's descriptions. Now she was here before him, in all her spectral beauty. For there was something ineffably beautiful about her, something tragically sad and appealing, despite her terrible condition – the smell that clung to her clothes and hair, along with the traces of grey dust and powder. Beneath it all, she was still a child.

Samuel followed her, not knowing where she was taking him, nor why.

Eliza lead him to the window and with a mournful expression pointed towards the family graveyard. Samuel followed the line of her gaze. The sleeve fell back from her white arm, barely-clad, revealing how mottled and pale the skin was. She must be so cold, and he had to suppress an urge to offer her his dressing-gown. Instead he looked at her and murmured, "Is that where you and your brother were buried? With the rest of your family?"

Eliza knitted her brow in confusion. Her voice, when it came, sounded pure and clear, like a distant bell. "I cannot recall exactly, but I do not think so."

"Where is it then ... the place where you are buried?"

Eliza looked at him sadly, but instead of replying she pointed vaguely towards the hills.

Samuel nodded encouragement. "Over there?"

She sighed heavily, as if the thought were unbearably painful to her, and drifted away. Samuel watched her go, feeling a strong urge to follow.

Missing

The fire had gone out sometime during the night and only ashes and burnt cinders remained.

Fiona groaned and stretched herself. "That was an uncomfortable night," she complained. "I think I prefer my own bed."

She slid out of her sleeping bag, muttering, "It's so cold."

"The power's still down by the looks of things," Sebastian said, trying one of the light switches.

"Oh great," she sighed. "The romance is beginning to wear off. I thought it would have been back on by now."

She knelt down in front of the hearth and began making an effort to get another fire going. Kindling, firelighters, scrunched-up newspapers and logs.

Granny Hughes looked in on them on her way downstairs. She grunted and shook her head. She was feeling miserable because of the cold and the extra work this would entail.

"Hello, Granny," Fiona called. "Did you sleep alright?"

"Aye. Right enough."

"The fire was cosy."

"Glad to hear it."

"But the power's still off."

"I noticed!" she responded. "Don't know how I'm supposed to cook and clean under these conditions," she muttered to herself, plodding down the stairs to begin work. The Aga ran on solid fuel, so she could keep the heat in, but ironing and vacuuming were out of the question.

The others began rolling up their sleeping bags and tidying up.

"Hey, where's Samuel?" Fiona asked suddenly. She'd only just noticed he was missing.

"Probably went downstairs to get some breakfast," Sebastian suggested. "Can't say I blame him. I'm starving."

But when they went downstairs to look, he wasn't there either.

"Have you seen Samuel, Granny?" Fiona asked.

She shook her head. "No, I haven't."

There was absolutely no sign of him. Fiona began to worry. She turned to her brothers and whispered "Where do you think he is?"

"I'm sure there's no need to panic," Sebastian said, sounding more confident than he felt. "He probably just went outside, or else he's already back home with his mum."

But Charles looked doubtful. Somehow he and Fiona just knew that wasn't the case. Both of them had met Eliza before and wondered what mischief she was capable of.

Fiona looked anxiously at her brother. "I'm scared, Charles," she admitted.

"Sebastian, go next door to the cottage and see if he's there," Charles instructed, looking straight at his brother. "But don't raise the alarm if he's not. We don't want Isabel getting worried."

"Come on with me, Fiona. We'll go and look in my room. After all, that's near their secret room, isn't it? She might decide to pay us another visit."

"You mean Eliza, don't you?" Fiona asked.

Her brother nodded. "Of course. Who else?"

"You don't think she's done something to him, do you?"

"Of course not," Charles assured his sister. "She's just a kid. She likes making mischief, that's all."

"So why the urgency?"

"I just want to find Samuel. Maybe she knows where he is."

At the cottage, Isabel was going through her morning ritual of re-lighting the stove.

"Oh Sebastian," she greeted him, when he turned up at the door. "How did the sleepover go?"

"Fine. We were really warm next to that fire."

"I bet you were. Lucky things. Did you sleep okay?"

Sebastian nodded vigorously, but said nothing.

There was an awkward silence. "Have you all had breakfast yet?"

"Er ... just about to," Sebastian muttered. It was obvious Samuel's mother had not set eyes on her son that morning.

"Well," she continued, "Samuel seems to have been and gone already, as his jacket and boots are gone from the porch and he didn't have them with him last night ... "Is everything okay?" she asked, noticing that Sebastian looked decidedly uncomfortable.

Rather than alarm her, Sebastian mumbled something incoherent, made his excuses and started to leave.

Just then, there was the sound of tramping footsteps and Samuel appeared in the doorway, laden with wood for the stove.

"Thought we might want this," he said, looking at the two of them. "Everything alright?"

"Yeah ... just wondered where you'd got to," Sebastian said hurriedly. "Breakfast's on the go in the kitchen if you want some," he added, glaring meaningfully at Samuel.

"Oh ... I woke early and thought I'd get this done before breakfast. I'll be over in a moment. Where d'you want this, Mum?"

Isabel watched Sebastian vanish under the archway to the house next door. *Something's up,* she thought. *Probably just kids' stuff.* Then, dismissing it from her mind, she headed off to her studio to start chiselling.

Charles and Fiona climbed the narrow stone stairs of the tower, trying to subdue any thoughts of panic.

"It'll be fine, Fiona. Honestly," Charles said.

But Fiona knew he couldn't be sure of that.

"He could be in danger," Fiona murmured. "And we don't even know where he is."

"Don't you think you're overreacting?" Charles asked. "We don't *know* he's been kidnapped by ghosts!"

Charles opened the door to his room, and stared at his computer desk. Clothes and books were strewn on the bed, the way he'd left them. This was where it had all started, when he began to write that terrible ghost story. The pages of his efforts were in evidence all over the desk.

"I wish I hadn't bothered with that ghost story now. It was rubbish, anyway."

"I doubt it was that which caused all this," Fiona pointed out, reading his thoughts.

She touched the keyboard gently. "It was Samuel and I who found the secret staircase, remember? But Eliza also said something about us seeing them in the tapestry."

"I first heard them behind this wall," Charles said, probing the wooden panelling with his hands. If there's a secret room behind there, we have to find it. We have to gain access somehow."

"But how?" Fiona cried. "We ought to tell Mum that Samuel's missing."

Charles hesitated. "We don't know that for sure yet."

"Yes ... we do, Charles. You know that we do."

Pounding footsteps sounded on the spiral staircase outside. Sebastian burst through the door.

"Samuel's fine. He went home. He'll be over for breakfast in a few minutes."

Charles looked at Fiona in relief.

"Told you," he said.

"You were right," she conceded. "My imagination's on overtime. It's being snowed in. It's driving me slightly mad."

"I'm starving," Sebastian interrupted. "Come on. Let's go."

From the shadows, Eliza watched them descend the staircase. *What did they think she had done?* she wondered sadly. *What mischief did they think she was capable of? She had wished Samuel no harm. They thought the worst of her, evidently.*

Blizzard

Over a delicious breakfast of hot pancakes, syrup and crispy bacon – courtesy of the solid fuel Aga – Samuel told the others of his adventures the night before.

"I couldn't sleep afterwards," he said. "I tried to, for ages. But it didn't work. So I just got up in the end and went for a walk instead, gathered wood for the stove. Thought I'd make myself useful."

"So she's appeared to you as well, now!" Fiona said. "So, we know we're not imagining things."

"We knew we weren't anyway!" Charles scoffed. "How much more proof do you need, if seeing with your own eyes isn't enough?"

"So what did she tell you?" Fiona asked Samuel eagerly.

"Not a lot, really," he replied. "She was very quiet. She just stood by the window, looking out, and pointing."

"At what?"

"The hills," he murmured, perplexed.

"Why?"

"I asked her where she was buried," Samuel said.

"And what did she say?"

"She said she wasn't sure. I don't think she really knew, for certain. At first, I thought she was pointing at the family graveyard."

"We could go there and find out," Fiona cried. "We could search the graves, read the inscriptions ... find out for sure."

"Well," Charles said, looking at the others. "I suppose we might get some answers that way."

"Fair enough," Sebastian said. "I can't think of any other plan."

"By the way," Charles added, "don't mention any of this to Granny. She'll only start chuntering on about frostbite and hypothermia."

With a hot breakfast inside their stomachs, they gathered noisily in the boot room to don plenty of layers, coats, scarves, boots, hats and mittens, until they looked like a group of Inuits.

"All we need now is a team of huskies," Samuel joked.

"Will Lucy do?" Fiona asked, as they ventured out into the freezing cold, trying to be cheerful, despite the gloomy nature of their expedition.

The snow had drifted and hardened overnight. Much to Granny Hughes's disappointment, it was impossible to get off the moor now. She disliked having to stay overnight at Dunadd, preferring to escape to her centrally-heated flat in town. Sometimes, if fate was on her side, she was snowed *out* rather than *in*, and couldn't make it up to the house to work for the Mortons. But not this time.

The weather outside was absolutely bitter, worse than the children had realised, and they were glad of the warm outer garments they'd put on. Lucy trotted beside them in the snow, wagging her tail enthusiastically. Fiona laid her hand on her back to feel the firm strength underneath. She was always such a good companion and it felt reassuring to touch something soft and warm.

"D'you think this is a good idea?" Charles asked suddenly, glancing up at the sky.

"We'll be fine. We're not going far," Samuel said. "We just have to find out where their graves are."

"He's right," Fiona said, her breath forming a white pearly mist in front of her face. "We have to find out."

The land around seemed unbelievably inhospitable and hostile under these conditions – no longer the safe playground they were used to. They could just make out the family graveyard in the distance, over the brow of the next hill, the graves all leaning like rotting teeth against the hillside, as bleak as could be. They were half-covered by snowdrifts, and the headstones were rather insignificant-looking, as if they had been buried here on a whim and half-forgotten. There was no sense of wanting to remember, no vaults or huge mausoleums commemorating the dead. If anything, the Morton family seemed to want to forget, burying their dead hastily and planting small headstones, to be stumbled upon almost by accident.

After trudging for what seemed like ages through the deep snow, the children reached their destination.

Fiona bent down and scooped snow from each tiny headstone, but there was no sign of the names they were looking for.

Samuel stood up straight and gazed into the middle distance.

"You know, I don't think they're buried here at all. Like she said … maybe they were buried elsewhere."

"We need to go back to the house," Charles suggested.

"Why?" Sebastian said. "It's stopped snowing now, and I – for one – want to keep on searching."

"Me too," Samuel said, remembering the forlorn expression on Eliza's face the night before and how his heart had gone out to her, even as her appearance filled him with dread.

They looked up towards the hills above Dunadd. When he had asked her about her grave, Eliza had pointed Samuel in the direction of the edge of the moor, but he didn't know exactly where she had meant.

"We could search?" Sebastian said desperately. "Use known landmarks."

"Landmarks?" Fiona said, looking out at the unending white before them. "Like what, exactly?"

"Fiona's right. It's too dangerous," Charles said.

"No, wait," Sebastian exclaimed triumphantly. "Do you remember that little ruin on the moor ... we used to go to it ... in the summer usually? A small chapel that was crumbling."

"That's right," Charles said, an earlier memory taking him back to a distant time, when their father was still alive. "It had no roof on it. It was a ruin ... a tiny little place."

"It's an obvious choice," Sebastian said. "We could try there. If this isn't where she's buried," he pointed at the leaning gravestones, "then it's bound to be the place. Has to be. Where else would she have meant, when she pointed at the hills?"

"It's definitely worth a try," Samuel said.

"As long as you know what you're doing," Charles cautioned. "Maybe I should come with you."

"They'll be fine," Fiona chided. "Sebastian knows this moor like the back of his own hand."

"But it's ages since we went to that chapel and everything looks different like this," Charles pointed out.

He surveyed the almost unrecognizable dips and hollows of the moor. Dunadd Woods stretched up darkly on the rise of the hill before them.

"We'll find it, no problem," Sebastian assured his brother, a steely determination showing in his face. It was good to see Sebastian so fired up by the project at last, after his earlier cynicism, so it was with reluctance that Charles agreed to a division of resources.

"Why don't you two carry on," Fiona suggested, "while Charles and I go back to the house? We can carry on with the hunt there?" She was conscious that there was still business to be attended to in Charles's room.

It seemed like a reasonable enough idea, in the end, despite Charles's reservations.

"Promise me you'll come straight back if it starts to snow again," he insisted before heading back to the house.

"We won't be gone long," Sebastian assured him. "If we don't find what we're looking for within the hour, we'll come home."

So Charles and Fiona retraced their steps back to the house, leaving the others to continue their search alone.

Samuel and Sebastian watched the tiny figures of Fiona and Charles disappear towards the comfort of Dunadd House, before beginning their long steady climb to Dunadd Wood. They walked in silence for a while, their faces impassive as they stared ahead at endless white.

"You are sure about this, aren't you?" Samuel asked his companion. "About there being a ruined chapel?"

"Of course I am."

"D'you think we're heading in the right direction?"

"Positive. I recognize the lie of the land ... and that copse just there." Sebastian pointed to a stand of trees, planted in the previous ten years or so: spruce, pine and Douglas fir, all dusted now with a fine sugar-coating of white powdery snow and ice. They trudged on, shoulders set firmly against the pitiless cold.

"It's like the Arctic," Samuel remarked, through his woollen scarf. "I always fancied going to Norway ... you know, to see the Northern Lights, but this is almost as good."

"You could go there one day, if you wanted to," Sebastian said.

"I suppose I could."

"You can see the Northern Lights from here sometimes. Not very much ... just a quick ribbon of light in the sky, like a rippling curtain. I didn't know what it was, at first, but Mum told me. It's a very rare thing, to see them this far south."

Without realizing it, they had wandered a considerable distance from their homes, and the house and outbuildings – including Samuel's cottage – were nowhere in sight.

"D'you think we will find their graves?" Samuel asked, glancing at the hills, so silent and still under their mantle of snow.

Sebastian didn't answer. He was fighting the creeping chill of unbearable cold that was beginning to invade his body. *Must keep moving*, he thought, and began beating his arms against the sides of his great padded jacket. "How many layers do you need in this place to keep warm? You know ... if Mum does decide to move, I hope she chooses the Caribbean next time."

"You don't mean that," Samuel said, laughing.

"Don't I?"

After walking for what seemed like ages, mindful of their promise to return within the hour, they finally stumbled upon the tiny blackened ruin, nestling against the edge of the forest. The little chapel looked abandoned and neglected, its roof open to the elements. Snow had piled up inside and swept against what remained of the broken altar-table. They stood at the entrance, looking in.

"Is it how you remember?" Samuel asked.

"Not exactly," Sebastian murmured. "It was a hot summer's day the last time I came here. We had a picnic."

"I wish we had one now ... a flask of tea, at any rate."

On the remaining walls were one or two grotesquely grinning gargoyles, disconcerting in appearance. Samuel stared at them, unnerved and fascinated. It seemed like a bad omen, somehow. Gravestones bent in the shadow of the tiny ruined chapel. It was possible to tell at a glance that there were carvings of skulls and crossbones on some of them, the ghastly death's head protruding through a light dusting of snow, scabbed all over with lichen and moss. Samuel shuddered. He stood in the snow, not really knowing how they'd got there, nor where they were. He was almost too cold and exhausted to think straight. The graveyard, he could see, was sheltered on two sides by a thick stand of trees so that the gravestones were not completely obliterated by the gathering snow. This allowed them to wipe away the white stuff that had drifted, and read the headstones ... one or two of them, at least.

They knelt, ignoring the cold and damp seeping into

their knees. Then they dug, using their gloved hands as shovels. It was easy to clear away the snow where it had drifted, because of the protection afforded by the sheltering copse of trees. Finally, after a while, they found what they were looking for.

"Here!" Samuel shouted. He sat back on his heels, triumphant.

Sebastian, who was working on another part of the little graveyard, abandoned his own gloomy efforts and headed towards Samuel.

Samuel was pointing to one headstone in particular.

There were two names chiselled into the sandstone, half-eroded by the elements, but still legible. *Eliza Morton. Born 1595. Died 1604*. Then below that: *John Morton. Born 1597. Died 1604.*

"This is where they're buried," Sebastian said. "We were right ... they must have died of the plague."

"But that still doesn't explain why they're haunting the house," Samuel mused.

"I wonder if their bodies are actually here or not?" Sebastian said ghoulishly. "The books said the plague victims were all buried and covered in lime ... remember?"

Samuel shuddered, recalling the chalky dust on Eliza's clothes, and quickly put the thought out of his mind.

"It's getting cold," Sebastian complained, rubbing his gloved hands together to ignite some warmth into them. "We should be getting back."

Samuel struggled up from his kneeling position to begin their journey home, reluctantly leaving the ruined chapel and its haphazard graveyard behind them.

They walked on for a minute or two in silence.

Samuel was wondering what exactly they would find, if they had the temerity to break open the graves where Eliza and John Morton were supposed to lie sleeping. Would they find them empty – as Sebastian had suggested? He pushed these grim thoughts aside. They were too horrible to even contemplate and he felt sickened by them. But his imagination had gone into overdrive. He couldn't stop thinking about it.

Then he found himself pulled up short, as he slammed straight into Sebastian's back. Sebastian had stopped walking and was standing stock still.

"Hang on ... where are we?"

Samuel was instantly alarmed by the worried note in Sebastian's voice – he who knew the moor so well.

"The cloud's come down."

He was right. The weather had changed almost without them noticing.

"We can't see anything. Where on earth has the house gone?"

They weren't even sure in which direction they were heading. They might as well have been spun round on the spot several times; they had no idea which way they were facing.

Then it hit them, as suddenly as a wall of ice, sweeping down unexpectedly from the high hills, as silent and lethal as a knife. A blizzard. An almost complete white-out, leaving them struggling and blinded.

Sebastian reached out and grabbed Samuel by the arm.

"So we don't get separated," he shouted, in explanation, "and lose each other."

They inched their way forward, as the blizzard whirled crazily all about them. It was terrifying to be aware suddenly of how dangerous and hostile this landscape could become, even when you knew it as well as Sebastian did. Every landmark, every familiar fence post, tree or distant hill was totally wiped out, masked from view. They might as well have been wading through soup. Nothing was visible, nothing at all. The boys were very frightened now.

In silence, they clung to each other, attempting to make their stumbling way forward.

"It's hopeless," Sebastian shouted. "If we keep walking we might end up wandering further from the house."

But if we stand still, we'll freeze. The words were on the tip of Samuel's tongue, but he refrained from saying them out loud.

They wandered blindly for some minutes more, until they found themselves up against a hard object of some kind. A lone tree, unprotected and desolate against the elements. They leaned against it for support and stood still, while the blizzard raged around them. When Samuel next attempted to move his foot, he saw that it had already become encrusted with snow, which had been swept against the side of his leg as if he were some immovable object, like a barn or the outbuildings.

If we're not careful, he thought, *we'll turn into a snowdrift ourselves, covered up for all eternity ... like the two children lost in the house.*

Sebastian didn't say it, but he was very afraid. He knew enough about the terrain around his home to understand that this could be their last and final resting place ... Bitterly, he began to regret his earlier enthusiasm and determination to find the ruined chapel. It had been misplaced confidence, always thinking he knew best. Then he thought sadly of what his family would have to say, when they found out he and Samuel were lost, and had not returned from their foolhardy expedition.

The kitchen at Dunadd was bustling and warm with

life. The dogs were crouching under the table, Granny Hughes was cooking so smells wafted deliciously down the passageway, and Mr Hughes was sitting down having a chat with Isabel Cunningham about the heating problem in her studio.

"It's hard to work in there when it's so cold."

"You could rig yourself up a nice little stove. There's an old one in the barn," Mr Hughes was telling her. "We could cut a hole in the roof and feed the vent through it."

"Would that work?"

"Like a treat. You could burn logs and coal in it, heat the place up nicely. Then you'd be warm even when the power's down."

Isabel stood up, encouraged by these thoughts. Her plans were looking up every day.

"Well, I'll let you good people get on then ..." and with that she went back to the cottage. At the back of her mind she was wondering where Samuel had gone and what he might like for tea tonight. Something warming like soup perhaps, with the weather closing in? It didn't occur to her to worry quite yet ...

Chris Morton was more than usually agitated.

"What is it, Mum?" Fiona asked.

"It's odd about the electricity, I keep thinking about it,

that's all," she admitted, distractedly. "For a minute there the other night, it was doing some really odd things. I'll call an electrician once the roads are clear again."

"You'd have thought it would've bin back on again by now, that's for sure," Granny commented, whisking one of the rabbits off the table. "Put that thing back in its cage," she instructed Fiona.

Fiona stood up, grabbing the rabbit under its belly. She swept it into an open cage on the worktop and sealed it shut. Then she glanced across the moor at the snowbound hills.

"That's odd."

"What is?"

Fiona had noticed lights glimmering through the thickening snowfall, just before the blizzard hit. "The Sheriffmuir Inn must have their power back. I saw their lights earlier."

Chris Morton came and stood beside her and peered out.

"Really? So, why don't we?"

"I wonder if Mr MacFarlane's been affected?" Fiona blurted out before she could stop herself. Her mother shot her a sharp look.

"Well, you're not going to visit him to find out," Chris Morton said. "The weather's closing in again. Look ... it's a virtual white-out out there!"

Granny Hughes agreed. "It's not good," she murmured. "All the same," Granny sighed. "Seems awfy strange."

She was right, but no one wanted to admit it. It seemed they were the only ones on Sheriffmuir without power.

Charles chose that moment to wander in from the hallway.

"Where are the other two?" his mother demanded.

He shook his head. "They should be back by now. They went out in the snow."

"They *what*?" Chris Morton exclaimed, unable quite to believe her ears. "What possessed them?" she cried.

"It was my fault," Charles stammered. "We ... we were looking for something."

"Yes. Looking for trouble," she snapped, but fear gripped her chest like a tightening vice.

Charles shook his head. "Fiona and I came back, and they promised they'd ..."

"Why on earth did you let them go off on their own?"

"We didn't think ... we thought ..."

"Exactly. You didn't think," his mother lashed out, in her rising panic.

"Now, now. Let's not lose our heads," Mr Hughes said.

"Maybe they're next door," Chris Morton muttered, looking out at the gathering maelstrom.

"Shall I go and look?" Fiona offered, getting up from the table.

"No, I'll go," Mrs Morton insisted. "You lot stay here."

Before they could stop her, she had buttoned up her padded jacket and pulled on her boots. From the kitchen window they watched her disappear between the trees, in search of Isabel.

Her fear increased with every footstep. She was beginning to get a bad feeling about this.

The Alarm is Raised

Above the clustered rooftops and tower of Dunadd, the snow clouds gathered, swirling endlessly in a confetti storm of white. It would have been pretty, if it wasn't so lethal; if two boys hadn't been out in it, lost on the hillside, not knowing which way to turn. How long before it got dark? Would the blizzard lift before then, or would it continue? Sheriffmuir was not a place to be out in after dark, particularly when a storm like this one hit. It was impossible to see more than two metres ahead, other than the shapeless forms of walls and shrubs. And Sebastian and Samuel were out there now, nowhere near the house. They had no landmarks or signposts to help them.

"What is it?" Granny demanded when Chris Morton returned soon after with Isabel. She could tell by the looks on their faces that something was desperately wrong. Isabel had searched the cottage and Chris Morton had stood outside in the blizzard, helplessly calling out the boys' names. Of course, there had been no response, other than a deafening silence.

"It's Samuel and Sebastian. They weren't at the cottage. They haven't come back."

Fiona and Charles exchanged worried glances.

"They're missing."

Fiona glanced towards her brother guiltily. He lowered his head, reading her thoughts. It was time to tell the truth. Or part of it, anyway. They were frightened of the consequences: of having withheld the truth in the first place, and for their brother and friend, lost out on the moor in the middle of a terrible blizzard.

"We know where they went," Charles blurted out, his face turning pale as all the adults turned to stare at him.

"What?" Isabel hissed, her voice dangerously quiet, as if she couldn't quite believe her ears.

"We know where they might have gone." He began nervously. "They went off in search of a graveyard, for something to do."

"Graveyard? What graveyard?" Isabel spat, confusion making her angry.

"It was after reading this book at the sleepover. We wanted to see if there really was a plague graveyard on Sheriffmuir, like the book said there was."

"Book?"

"This book we found ..." Fiona explained "... in the

library. We were just reading up about it. Charles and I went along too. The weather was fine earlier, no snow or anything. Then Charles and I decided to come home 'cos we thought it was too much for Lucy, and the others... well, they decided to keep looking. We thought they'd be alright. We didn't think there'd be a blizzard or anything."

She exchanged nervous glances with her brother. Once again, they had omitted to tell the whole truth. They hadn't mentioned the ghostly apparition that had pointed them in the direction of the graveyard in the first place.

But they had said enough to terrify the adults into radical action.

Mr Hughes and Chris Morton volunteered to walk to the Inn to raise the alarm, but Isabel insisted that she went instead.

Granny protested. "The weather's awful. You'll be lost an' all. You can't see a thing out there." But Mr Hughes reassured her.

"If we stick to the road we can't go wrong. We'll just follow the fence along the driveway."

"You should stay here in case Samuel comes back," Chris implored Isabel, but Isabel would not hear of it.

"One of us needs to get help and someone has to stay here," she said practically.

Isabel set off through the snow, accompanied by a faithful Mr Hughes, who endeavoured all the time to reassure her.

Fiona and her brother watched them go with foreboding in their hearts.

Although Sebastian and Samuel had gone in the opposite direction, in search of the ruined chapel, the adults decided that it would be better to get more professional help involved in the search, rather than try and find them themselves.

"That's our best bet," Mr Hughes had told them. "We'll be no use to the boys if we get lost up there ourselves."

"He's right," Granny urged everyone. They stood at the window, looking out in fear.

At the Inn the power was on, but the telephone cables were down. However, the owners managed to get a signal on their mobile and called for help. The police and rescue services promised to attend, but the road was completely blocked, so this would prove difficult.

The staff at the Inn tried to calm down Isabel with comforting words and offers of sweet tea, but she waived them all aside. All she wanted was her son. Up at the house, Chris Morton was enduring a similar anguish. Both mothers waited ... in torment.

The hours ticked by, and Isabel began to entertain the possibility of Samuel being lost on the freezing moor overnight. How would he survive? Periodically, they tried to ring Chris Morton at the house to see if Samuel and Sebastian had turned up there, safe and well, putting an end to the whole unbelievable nightmare; proving that it had all been a silly mistake, after all, but there was still no signal on the mobile. No one answered at the house.

A little later they switched the radio on and Isabel listened in stoical silence to the following report.

"Fears are growing for the safety of two young boys missing on Sheriffmuir since late this afternoon. They were last seen at around lunchtime, but failed to return home after going out to try to find an old graveyard. It is believed that the boys, aged 12 and 13, may have wandered off onto the moor. The alarm was raised when Samuel Cunningham and Sebastian Morton were reported missing by their families early this evening. Efforts to organize a search party have been hampered by the severe weather. A helicopter cannot be sent out at present owing to the white-out conditions and low cloud, severely hampering visibility. Rescuers are hoping that the boys have enough sense to have taken shelter somewhere."

Isabel leant forward and switched the radio off. She

stared into the roaring fire. Mr Hughes sat nervously beside her, trying to offer support.

"It'll be fine, so it will," he murmured kindly, patting her hand. "Take a sip of tea now. It'll do you good."

Isabel shook her head in silence. Her heart had been gripped by panic at hearing her son's name mentioned on the radio in that context. A mother's worst fears had been realized. She couldn't believe this was happening to her ... or to Chris either. What must she be feeling like, back at the house, waiting for news? The two women had never dreamt anything like this would happen when they had sat together in the drawing room the other night, sharing a bottle of wine as they watched the children toast bread in front of the fire. Their lives had been turned upside down in a matter of minutes, as they realized the boys were missing.

The reality of it hit Isabel with terrible force. She had been trying to pretend that none of this was happening, that it was all some elaborate joke, and the boys would suddenly turn up, safe and well; Samuel telling her he'd just been sledging with Sebastian.

But she knew that wasn't going to happen.

This was no sledging weather.

Dark Encounters

Meanwhile, back at the house, Fiona and Charles sat upstairs gazing out the window, waiting for the blizzard to lift. But it didn't. It simply went on swirling, as Sheriffmuir grew darker and darker.

"Maybe one of us should have gone out looking for them?" Fiona said anxiously.

"What good would that do? We'd only get hopelessly lost. We can't do that to Mum. She's upset enough as it is."

"We can't just sit here and do nothing," she cried. She was tugging on her hair nervously, a habit she adopted if she was distressed about anything.

"Will you stop doing that?" Charles said.

"What?"

"Your hair?"

"Oh."

But she kept on doing it all the same. It gave her some kind of comfort.

They were sitting in Charles's room, up in the tower.

Normally, Fiona would never hang around in the boys' rooms, but this was different. The brother and sister, normally quite distant with each other, were seeking solace in one another's company. Charles stared at the blank computer screen on his desk. For him, this was where it had all started, with that stupid ghost story he'd been trying to write. *Shiver*. Could words be so powerful that they could make things happen? That was nonsense and he knew it. Maybe his opening sentence had been more effective than he realized.

"We could try to find out more about the graveyard," Fiona cried out suddenly, on an impulse. "Find out where exactly it is?"

"What difference would that make? Samuel and Sebastian are lost. We still wouldn't know where to find them."

"No, but it would give us a clue."

But Charles was sunk in gloom and no amount of conjecturing on Fiona's part could lift his spirits. He blamed himself for letting this happen, for allowing the other two to wander off on their own.

"I knew it was a stupid idea," he muttered.

"I know," Fiona comforted him. "But you did try to tell them. It's not your fault."

There was a short silence, while the snow built up against the window-panes.

"We could try to find Eliza," Fiona suddenly suggested, "... get her to tell us where the graveyard is?"

Charles glanced across at his sister. "I suppose it would take our mind off things. There's no use sitting here, worrying. That's not going to help anyone, is it?"

"Exactly," Fiona said.

So, under cover of darkness, they began a search of their own, furiously examining every gloomy corner, corridor and attic of the house they knew so well. They left no stone unturned, no possible avenue unexplored. They would not give up.

Night had properly fallen. And still Samuel and Sebastian hadn't returned. The Wharry Burn muttered quietly beneath its blanket of snow and ice. The winter before had been so severe that even the fast-flowing waterfall near Mr MacFarlane's farmhouse had fallen silent and turned into an ice sculpture. At least temperatures hadn't dropped quite that far, yet.

There was a possibility the boys could survive the night, if they had found somewhere to shelter. Last year that would not have been remotely possible. No one would have survived a night outside in temperatures of minus twenty degrees. How resourceful were the boys? Their families hoped they were extremely resourceful. But what if one of them had met with an accident? The nagging, worrying thoughts swirled about as pitilessly as the snowstorm itself. It was no use speculating. They simply had to sit and wait and let the emergency services do their job.

No one could sleep. They all sat round the kitchen table, fretting. Isabel had returned with Mr Hughes and was resting in a downstairs room on a makeshift divan. The power had not returned, so they were making do with candles again. Mr Hughes lit fires in some of the major rooms, but they were battling with the cold on all fronts.

As the two families went about their business, lighting fires and dealing with the current state of emergency and the loss of power, Eliza watched from the shadows. She saw Granny tucking Isabel up under a blanket. She saw Charles and Fiona search the library upstairs, the landing and the attics, probing into places they had never noticed before. She saw them watch and worry and listen for every sound, hoping against hope that it was the boys returning.

She ran along the top landing of the house, a pattering of feather-light footsteps, and laughed to herself. Fiona and Charles heard her – or thought they heard her – and raised their heads briefly.

Nodding at Charles, Fiona stood up and went to investigate.

Her brother followed her and they stood beside the old grandfather clock, staring up into the dark void of the house above, before starting to climb the spiralling staircase.

"Did you hear that noise earlier?" Fiona whispered.

Charles nodded.

Fiona looked resolute. "It was her. I'm sure of it."

"D'you think the adults heard it?"

Fiona shook her head. "They're too worked up to notice anything. I'm going to find her. She must know where Samuel and Sebastian are."

"How do you know?"

"Isn't it obvious? She told Samuel about the graveyard in the first place ... remember? Maybe she can help us by telling us where to look."

Although they hadn't realized it, Lucy, Fiona's favourite Labrador, had followed them up the stairs. They took comfort from this. She had always been an excellent guard dog, warning them of any unseen presence. She would take care of them. With slow but intrepid determination, they mounted the stairs in darkness.

As they reached the upstairs landing, the dog began to release a low ominous growl. Fiona put her fingers into Lucy's fur and gently comforted her. "It's alright, girl. Nothing to worry about."

She kept her hand on Lucy's neck and they crept along the deserted corridor.

The house seemed unnaturally quiet. No sign of life anywhere.

Not for the first time it occurred to Fiona that she'd prefer to live in Samuel's tiny cottage, with its manageable spaces, rather than this great lofty pile with its unopened doors and huge empty rooms. She loved Dunadd, but sometimes it frightened her too.

They encouraged Lucy to accompany them as they approached the drawing room. A floorboard creaked inside the far room.

"What was that?" Charles hissed.

"We know you're here," Fiona uttered to the shadows around them. But there was no answering whisper.

The house had always made strange noises in the night, ever since she could remember: radiators ticking – when the power was connected, that is; floorboards and doors creaking; the boiler firing up; mice scuttling about behind the wooden panelling or up in the attic. It was just the normal night-time activity of any old house.

They pushed the door open and crossed the drawing room. Lucy suddenly pulled away from Fiona's grasp. They heard her claws clicking against the wooden floorboards. The dog stood near the half-open door of the library, ears flattened, body tense and growling.

Fiona and Charles followed her, and slowly pushed the library door wider. It creaked eerily on its hinges, sending shivers down their spines. Suddenly, they heard another scurry of movement. Eliza stood behind the desk, as if using it as a shield or barrier between herself and them. She stared at them across the room, her eyes bright and fiery ... feverish. There was a challenge in those eyes, as if daring them to defy her, to take her on. After all, they were given to thinking the worst of her and she knew it. She didn't care what they thought now. Let them think what they liked.

Fiona got straight to the point. "Our brother, Sebastian, and Samuel ... do you know where they are?"

Charles put a steadying hand on Fiona's arm, warning her not to antagonize Eliza. It would do no good to upset her.

Eliza put her head on one side, as if she did not understand the question. "Why dost thou ask me that?"

"They went to try and find your grave," Fiona persisted. "You and your brother's. They haven't come home. Where did you send them?"

"I sent them nowhere," Eliza replied. "Why dost thou accuse me? Thou art very impertinent to say so."

Fiona stared at the little girl in disbelief, this

pathetic but ghostly apparition which hovered before them, causing mischief and yet purporting to be innocent of any crime.

"They could be in trouble," Fiona cried. "They could be dead."

Eliza stared back.

"There's a blizzard out there," Fiona went on. "If they don't come home tonight, they may never come home again."

The little girl's face had turned serious, realization slowly dawning. "I canst tell thee not where they are. I know not."

"But you can tell us where the graveyard is?"

"Which one?"

"The one where you were buried ... beside the little chapel on the moor. The chapel, which is now a ruin."

Eliza looked blank. "I know not where we were buried. It is not certain we were buried at all. It is all so confusing in my mind. Thou makest me sad, speaking so ..."

The little girl had a way of melting back into the shadows, making herself invisible on a whim.

"Wait. Don't go," Fiona begged. "We need to find them. We need you to help us."

But Eliza had not disappeared. She was beckoning to someone invisible, who lurked near the secret entrance in the fireplace.

"John," she muttered. "Come out where they can see you."

"No, I dare not," a boy's voice whimpered, so quietly that Fiona and Charles weren't sure if they had heard him.

"John, wouldst thou have them take you for a coward?" Eliza demanded, more impatiently this time.

"Yes," came a small voice in reply.

Fiona looked past her into the shadows and gloom of the library, but she could see nothing of a ghost boy, too frightened and nervous to show himself. But she heard his next words clearly.

"Eliza, let us go back to our room."

"What room?" Fiona demanded, quick as a flash.

"The room they boarded up ..." Eliza said, "after we died."

"How do we get to that room?" Charles asked.

"Thou canst not," Eliza said simply. "Not unless thou becomst like us. It is on the other side."

"The other side of what?" Fiona begged.

What terrible secrets did these mysterious ghostly children, forlorn and forgotten, have in their possession? Fiona longed to ask them about it, but part of her was afraid to know the answer.

"Thy mother will have to leave this house," the girl

predicted, staring at Fiona with grim satisfaction. "Tell her, John," she cried, her voice becoming shrill. "Tell her what will happen."

"I do not know what will happen, Eliza," a small disembodied voice whimpered. "I want to go back to bed, to sleep, until the nightmare be over ... at last."

"Why did they board up the room you died in?" Fiona insisted.

"Because they wanted to forget," Eliza hissed. "They wanted to forget Eliza Morton and her brother, John, because of what happened to us. But we have always been here. Waiting."

There was a terrible silence, while Fiona and her brother allowed these awful words to sink in.

"Waiting for what?" she asked.

But Eliza refused to answer. She turned and left the room, leading her brother by the hand. For a brief moment, Fiona saw them both as dim outlines. The boy was much smaller than his sister, more vulnerable-looking; his face was peevish and sad.

"You haven't told us where they are ..."

A faint voice replied, "Worry not. It is not their time. They will return."

Then they were gone.

Eliza and John made their way back to their secret lair:

their refuge. The little boy sat down on the dusty floor and began to play with his wooden soldiers again. Cobwebs draped the beds like a shawl to keep the ghosts warm. Ruined books spilled out from the one bookshelf, their leaf-brown pages spotted with mildew and damp, almost unreadable.

John glanced across at his older sister with eyes that were forever mournful.

"I do not feel very well," he whimpered softly.

Eliza ignored him.

The boy shivered inside his loose cotton shift. Ghosts were not supposed to feel the cold, but John felt it all the time. He remembered how his mother had left him alone so often with Eliza and wished now that she had been around more; that she had comforted him the way he had seen Chris Morton comfort her children in the rooms downstairs. Eliza and he had always been alone. For almost as long as he could remember. There had been a time before, when more people had been around. He recalled it dimly, but the memories were getting fainter and fainter. This is the way it would always remain now. Just he and Eliza, alone in the shadowy gloom of a house that grew more decrepit with age and was filled with echoes from a past that only they could hear.

An Empty Graveyard

A stiff breeze blew across the surface of the snow, whipping up powdery spirals that danced and zigzagged towards them. The two boys stared out at the frozen wastes, afraid to admit to each other that they were well and truly lost. The hills around them were eerily empty. The lowering cloud had removed all landmarks, and the blizzard had obliterated all trace of their own footsteps, so that they couldn't even see where they had come. They had come too far and they knew it. They had disobeyed the sensible rules of conduct, which apply when it comes to walking in the Scottish hills. People died up here. Both boys knew this.

Samuel breathed on his gloved fingers to keep them warm, glancing across at Sebastian.

They wandered about helplessly for a bit, making sure not to lose sight or hold of each other, for that would have been fatal indeed. To be alone in this frozen waste did not bear thinking about. They had obviously wandered in the wrong direction when the blizzard came down, and had strayed further and further from Dunadd.

"I haven't got a clue where we are," Sebastian called.

"Me neither. Maybe when the blizzard clears ..." Samuel suggested vaguely.

But the weather didn't seem to want to oblige. It had no intention of blowing itself out, but raged on and on, until a new threat lingered. It began to get dark. Night was fast approaching.

"We need to find somewhere to shelter," Sebastian stated.

Samuel nodded, too weary and exhausted to do anything else.

They struggled on through the anonymous landscape, aware that they were much higher than they should be. Sebastian knew he had a box of matches in his pocket. He could feel it digging into his trouser leg. If they could just find somewhere to shelter. He regretted now leaving the graveyard behind and the little ruined chapel. They could have sought refuge inside its walls, broken as they were. It would at least have offered some respite, from the wind and the chill.

Suddenly he was aware that Samuel had stopped. For one awful moment, he panicked, thinking he'd lost him.

"What? What is it?"

"Look here," Samuel called. He had almost missed it as they waded through the swirling eddying curtain of snow, but here, set in the hillside, was an overhang of rock, and beneath it was a cave.

They ventured inside and immediately found themselves somewhat protected from the biting wind. The snow was falling in such a way that it didn't penetrate the opening. They struggled further in on their hands and knees. Neither spoke. This was survival at its worst. They knew their lives depended on their own skill, and both of them were concentrating on seeing out the night without perishing in the cold. Sebastian took out the box of matches with trembling fingers. Samuel watched him in silence, then found some brushwood at the back of the cave ... just enough to start a fire. Sebastian struggled to handle the spindly sticks, but finally the match took, and he held the tiny flame to the gathered scrub and rubbish in the corner, whatever they could salvage for a fire. It flared up for a few seconds, then crackled away merrily. The boys huddled close, the bright light playing over their faces in the gloom.

"It won't last long," Sebastian said.

In response, Samuel pulled another bundle of tinder from the back. At some point, someone had cleared the land nearby of bracken and fern, thorn and scrub, dumping it unceremoniously at the back of the cave. Either that, or it had been swept there over time, by wind and weather, after the local shepherd had left the stuff in a tidy pile. It's what usually happened with anything left lying on the moor.

The boys were miserable and frightened.

"You know what it says in my survival handbook, don't you?" Samuel said. "We need each other's body warmth to stay alive."

They wrapped their arms about each other, and tended the little fire as best they could.

"And we mustn't fall asleep," Sebastian warned. "Whatever you do, don't close your eyes."

But it was hard not to, with the fusty warmth beginning to fill the cave. The rocky overhang protected them from the worst of the bitter wind, but they were frozen. Their mutual body warmth was helping. They just had to survive the night.

"If we can make it till morning," Sebastian said, "the blizzard might have stopped, and we can find our way home."

But the morning seemed a million miles away, and meanwhile they felt utterly desolate, wondering if they would ever see their homes again, or if they would die here, mummified in a frozen tomb until someone found them in the spring.

When dawn at last penetrated their temporary den, they couldn't believe they had made it. They were still alive. Back at the house, they knew their families must be fearing the worst, for who could survive a night like that out in the open? It was still early. The sun rose above the edge of the moor, chasing the shadows away and sparkling on the blanket of snow, which rippled and undulated as far as the eye could see. The rising sun stained the far hills pink and blue, and even in their terrible state, they couldn't help noticing its beauty. It was a miraculous dawn for the two boys.

Sebastian peered out from the mouth of the cave. "It's stopped snowing," he announced, unnecessarily. The blizzard had worn itself out or gone elsewhere, leaving behind a transformed landscape.

"What now?" Samuel asked.

Sebastian shrugged. "Start heading for home?"

They peered all around them: endless white in all directions, with no sign of Dunadd House.

"I suppose if we just keep heading downwards, we can't go wrong," Sebastian murmured. "What d'you think?"

Samuel shrugged. They were reluctant to leave the relative warmth and shelter of their cave. It had been a long night, fearing the worst, facing whatever demons had confronted them. They had needed all their strength and bravery to survive it. Emerging into the open, they began their walk as the light grew brighter in the sky.

It was hard-going. They weren't really sure which direction they were heading in. They might have missed Dunadd altogether and be heading for a different part of Sheriffmuir entirely. They had no way of knowing. Nothing looked familiar. There was no sign of the little ruined chapel, nor its huddle of neglected graves. The hills were a confusing place, especially when covered in snow. You could end up going in circles for hours, never getting to where you needed to be.

But the boys kept going. The wind had whipped across the surface of the snow all night, drifting, so that their own footprints had disappeared, as well as any others that might have been of help. They struggled on in the direction they hoped Dunadd House lay, using the position of the sun as a vague guide.

Finally, halfway through the morning, after what seemed like an eternity of wading through endless white, Samuel stopped and pointed. He could see the rise of Dunadd Wood below them, and beyond that, a familiar tower peeping above the trees. Dunadd House sat like a ship on an ocean, indomitable ... waiting for them.

They began to run in their relief, leaping over the drifts and dunes of snow. At the same moment they heard a helicopter circling in the sky above them. They stood still and waved their arms above their heads.

In the sky above, the helicopter banked and swung round, returning the way it had come. The pilot and one of his companions pointed to where they could see two tiny dark figures stumbling through the snow, laughing and crying with relief. The boys had been spotted. The rescue was called off.

The whole family were at the breakfast table when they heard the commotion outside. No one had any appetite. Granny had insisted on putting down some toast and cereal, but the children toyed with it, and both Isabel and Chris had point-blank refused to eat. The helicopter was making a terrific din overhead, whipping up the snow into sparkling spirals on the ground outside. Then they heard other noises – shouts, laughter and whooping.

Fiona leapt up and ran to the window, where she saw her brother and her best friend, running and stumbling towards the house, almost falling over in their haste and exhaustion.

"They're here," she screamed, shouting over her

shoulder to the rest of them. "It's Samuel and Seb. They've come home." She flung open the door and ran across the snow towards them, with the helicopter circling like an eagle above them.

The household erupted. Everyone was talking at once. Isabel almost fainted with relief, and Granny had to revive her with old-fashioned, but still effective, smelling salts. Isabel spluttered and coughed.

"Are you trying to kill me?"

Charles laughed, patting Granny on the shoulder.

The news was put out that the boys had turned up, safe and sound, and a wave of relief swept through the entire household, extending to the local community beyond. At the inn they received the news with a cheer, for the worst had been feared and everyone had been dreading the morning and what they might find. The nightmare was over.

Almost ...

"I couldn't believe it when I saw you walking towards the house," Fiona cried. "I wasn't sure if it was really you."

"How on earth did you manage?" Chris murmured, administering hot cups of tea and blankets. Samuel and Sebastian didn't think they'd ever been more delighted to see a lit stove in their lives before. Granny threw the metal door open, and they sat before the

Aga, pulling their chairs up close to benefit from the glowing heat within.

"We found a cave," Samuel said. "We didn't think we'd last the night."

"We tried to build a small fire, but it didn't last long, so we kept close for warmth."

"And tried not to fall asleep."

"And did you?" Fiona asked.

"I don't remember."

"Leave the boys alone, Fiona," her mother urged. "They must be tired."

Although explanations would be required later.

"Whatever possessed you Sebastian?" his mother demanded at last, her temper getting the better of her finally. "Wandering off like that in this weather?"

"We were looking for something."

"So your brother said. Looking for a graveyard or some such nonsense ..."

Isabel was gazing at Samuel as if she thought he might melt away before her very eyes. All those long hours spent in her studio, partially neglecting him while she worked away at her art, and now she felt as if she never wanted to lose sight of him again.

"I'm such a bad parent," she sobbed, in relief and gratitude.

"Don't be silly, Isabel," Chris scolded her gently.

"You're not a bad parent. We all do our best. It's all we can do."

"Tch!" Granny said. "Don't take on so. The boys are safely home now and let's be thankful for that. It could have all turned out very differently."

"Yes, yes, Granny," Chris Morton said, trying to change the subject. "Well, I must say you were very sensible in taking shelter like that. You did the right thing in the circumstances."

Questions would have to be asked ... and answered, but one thing was certain ... whatever else the children told their parents in explanation, there was one piece of information they still weren't ready to impart ... the appearance of Eliza Morton and her timid little brother. Despite everything, they didn't want to give Mrs Morton any reason to leave Dunadd. The recent crisis itself was enough to be going on with.

Samuel was bundled up in blankets and Isabel was determined to sweep him off back to the cottage as soon as possible, but he refused.

"I want to stay here," he said, "for now."

"Maybe it's for the best," Chris suggested. "I'll make up a bed for you in a spare room," she told Isabel. "You can stay here too, obviously." For it was clear that there was absolutely no way that Isabel was leaving the house without her son.

"Questions can wait until the morning," Chris Morton said.

Fiona and Charles were not prepared to wait that long before finding out what had happened to the boys.

"Where were you?" Fiona asked him, once they were alone.

Samuel shook his head. "I haven't a clue. We were so lost. At first it was fine ... we found the ruined chapel."

"And their graves too," Sebastian cut in.

"You did?" Fiona and Charles listened in amazement, as the boys described scraping the snow off the sandstone to reveal the names of John and Eliza Morton.

"It gave the dates of their births and deaths," Samuel said. "But nothing else."

"Nothing?" Fiona repeated, in disappointment. "There was nothing about how they might have died ... no affectionate message from their loving relatives ...?"

Samuel shook his head. "No. Just the bare brutal facts. But it's a plague graveyard, alright. There are skull and crossbones on most stones."

"How do we explain any of this to our mothers?" Fiona sighed.

"We don't," Charles said. "Not yet."

The others silently agreed.

A Taste for Mischief

All was quiet in the house. After the excitement of the past few hours, everyone was at last sleeping. Eliza paused at the head of the staircase and surveyed the gloom beneath her. She loved the chaos she created, the fear she inspired.

The blizzard had left a completely white moor behind. Eliza could see it all shining beyond the window, where the house cast its great black shadow against the snow. The boys had settled down to their cosy comfortable lives again, after their adventure. Eliza envied them. Their life was so simple compared with her lonely fate. She had only her brother for company and he cried most of the time. He still missed their mother, although their mother was long since dead. Nothing could bring her back. Not the way *they* had come back ... she and John.

If they opened those graves where our names are carved, Eliza thought – and had said as much to Fiona – *they would find no bodies. Just empty graves. Our bodies were flung into a plague pit, a communal grave where no one knew our identities. Rich and poor alike were flung there; tossed without care or ceremony.* These were her terrible thoughts, her terrible memories, as she drifted from floor to floor, claiming the house as her own.

The little girl was learning to entertain herself. She was playing tricks, having some fun.

When she heard someone approach on the staircase beneath, she melted back into the shadows, ethereal and weightless. She managed to blend softly with the air around her. It was quite a skill and she was getting rather good at it.

Chris Morton was climbing the stairs back to her room, her tread heavy with fatigue. She had been downstairs to fetch a glass of milk, after being woken by a nightmare of some kind. The little girl watched in silence.

She was fascinated by mothers and the idea of mothers, especially since she and her brother had been without one for so long. She had had occasion to observe that the children who lived in this house seemed to be well cared for. They didn't have to cry themselves to sleep at night, nor comfort a little brother who wouldn't stop wailing.

Making herself invisible, Eliza drifted as close as she dared to Chris Morton and stared right through her. For a moment Mrs Morton felt a cold chill pass through her body. She dropped her cup by mistake and it smashed against the floor.

"Oh," she cried, and began to dab at her dressing-gown with a tissue. "How clumsy."

She cleared up the mess as best she could and retreated to her room, but as she closed the door behind her, she was almost sure she saw a child's shadow slip sideways across the hall. Pausing for a moment, she shook her head. She must be imagining things, she decided, and went wearily towards her bed.

However, she spent a restless night, her thoughts returning to the past. How strange that they should have found a secret staircase in that very room: the library which she had always feared. Since her husband's untimely death, she had brought up her three children all alone in this great house, determined to stay put for posterity's sake, despite the loneliness and isolation. She loved it, in a way ... she did ... but it had its drawbacks.

One of those drawbacks was hovering outside the door right now, although Chris Morton did not know it. Eliza floated, bodiless almost, across the hall to Fiona's room. She would not wake them this time. No, the house was all hers. This family might think they owned it: they slept in its beds, occupied its rooms, ate from its tables, warmed themselves before its fires ... but it really belonged to her and her little brother, John. They possessed the house in a way that no living being could ever understand. They knew the way that every stair creaked, the worn tread on a polished board, the touch and feel of a solid doorknob beneath the hand. They had memorized it all, feeling it now through their papery bodies, as if they were books full of information, containing every nuance and domestic detail of Dunadd House. Her brother John was reluctant to join her on these jaunts of hers, but he would ... in time. She would encourage him slowly.

She looked up to see a familiar figure standing at the end of the corridor, staring at her.

John.

She floated towards him, lightly taking his hand. "We are here to stay," she whispered to her brother. "This is our house, John. No one else's. It belongs to thee and me."

John gazed at her. He relied on Eliza. She was his mentor, his only friend. The only person he could turn to when he was sad. And he was sad ... all the time.

"What will we do now?" he asked, his voice so small and fragile in the silence.

Eliza looked at him and laughed. "That which we have always done. We wait. We watch and we wait ..."

Below them, the grandfather clock marked the passage of time, its notes filling the void.

Nightmare

Charles woke up in a sweat. He had dreamt that Dunadd was a burnt-out ruin. He could see right inside the house as if he was hovering above it. All of the rooms had been destroyed and smoke coiled from the charred remains. The spiralling staircase was open to the sky and snow drifted in, sweeping up against the large stone fireplaces, which had survived the fire. Flames had swept through the edifice, gobbling it up like a hungry monster, until there was almost nothing left: just an empty, smoking shell.

He sat up and looked around him, half expecting to see flames licking the walls and the oak panelling ... and breathed a sigh of relief. Only a dream, he told himself.

The next day dawned bright and clear. No more snow was forecast and Granny Hughes even began to entertain thoughts of making another attempt to return to her centrally-heated flat in the village. The adults were dying to ask Samuel and Sebastian some questions. No one knew what to make of their foolhardy expedition, but for now they were simply glad that the boys were safe and well.

Patrick MacFarlane stood looking up at the gleaming windows of Dunadd, broken blinds hanging askew in the library. The place was getting more and more neglected by the day. He could see at a glance that Chris Morton was struggling to maintain the place since her husband died.

He shook his head and approached the house.

The dogs barked at his arrival, but wagged their tails sheepishly when they saw him.

Granny Hughes came into the passageway and ushered him in.

"I was beginning to wonder if you were still alive," Granny remarked, as he followed her into the kitchen.

"Aye, just about," he muttered. "I heard the reports on my wee transistor." He paused and cleared his throat. "I was concerned an' all. Are they back?"

Fiona leapt up from the table, and put her arms round the old man. Chris Morton encouraged him to take a seat.

"No, no. I'll not stop. You'll have enough trouble to be dealing with."

"For goodness sake, man. Stay an' have a cuppa with us. You'll be needing it after your walk from the house," Granny scolded.

"Aye, well ... I'll not say no." He ruffled Samuel's hair.

"Glad to see you're safely back, lads. You've had us all fairly worried, so you have."

Samuel blushed.

"They still have a few questions to answer, mind," Granny added.

"Now, Granny," Chris Morton cut in. "Leave them be. They've been through enough. We're just glad to have them home, aren't we, Isabel?"

Isabel nodded her relief, dropping a kiss on the top of her son's head.

"Mum!" he protested. "Not in public."

Mr MacFarlane laughed, as he sat down to drink his tea.

"Men don't like a fuss, do we boys?" he said. "When will women learn, eh?"

Ignoring this comment, Fiona leapt up and grabbed the old man by the arm. "I nearly forgot. We've got something to show you."

"Let the man drink his tea," Granny scolded.

"It's alright ... the tea can wait," Mr MacFarlane responded, allowing himself to be led out of the kitchen and up the spiralling staircase to the rooms above. Isabel, Granny Hughes and Chris Morton stayed behind in the kitchen.

After they'd left the room, Granny shot a furtive glance across at Mrs Morton. "He's a lovely man, so he is."

Chris nodded. "I suppose you're right."

"The kids love him, anyway." Granny banged a saucepan of cabbage down on the draining board with a thud. "Wonder if he wants to stay for lunch?"

"We'll ask him when he comes down," Mrs Morton said.

Granny, pleased with herself, allowed a rare smile to play around her lips but kept her back to the rest of the room so the others couldn't tell. She didn't hold with open displays of emotion and there had been far too many of those recently.

Up in the library, Fiona, Samuel and the two older boys led Mr MacFarlane towards the great stone fireplace set into the wall of the narrow room. They pressed the servant's bell so that he could watch the huge stone slide sideways, revealing the hidden staircase behind it. He was suitably impressed.

"So, what else has been happening?" he asked them quietly. "Other than your recent capers on the moor, of course. What were you doing out there, by the way?" he asked.

No one could avoid giving Mr MacFarlane a straight answer.

"We were looking for their graves," Samuel admitted. "We had this sleepover and Eliza appeared to me while the others were asleep. She pointed me in that direction, but didn't seem sure if they were really buried there."

"I remembered a little ruined chapel from a long time ago," Sebastian added, "and we thought it might be the place Eliza meant ... so ..."

"So you ended up forgetting the time, wandering off and being caught out in a blizzard?"

The boys nodded.

"Well, at least you're safe," the old man murmured. "You had me worried sick when I heard the news."

"We haven't told Mum about it yet ... not all of it." Fiona looked at Mr MacFarlane. "What do you think?" she asked him then. "About Eliza and her little brother?"

The old man sighed. "What do I think?" He paused and was silent for a moment. "I think ... the dead are best left in peace."

The children looked at him in disappointment. It was not what they wanted to hear, but it was true.

"If their graves are empty, then so be it. There is nothing we can do about that."

Fiona shook her head. "You're wrong," she cried. "We could find the secret room. We could find out whether or not they were flung into a plague pit, and what happened to them."

Mr MacFarlane looked at her. "And once you have found out all the information you can ...? What then?"

She hesitated. "Then we'll know," she said, defensively, her voice wavering a little as the others looked at her.

"Know what?"

"We'll know what happened to Eliza and her brother."

"And will knowing make any difference to the children? Or to yourselves?"

Samuel spoke up for the first time, defending the desperate attempts of his friend to hold her ground against the old man's reasoning. "Knowledge always makes a difference," he said.

Mr MacFarlane nodded. "Good answer. But is it the right one?"

They concluded their discussion, with nothing more to say on the subject. Mr MacFarlane knew nothing about any plague pits nearby. Hunger at last drove them downstairs, but it was an uneasy Fiona who sat before her meal that lunchtime, mulling over all that had been said, still desperate for answers. She was not prepared to let sleeping dogs lie. Nor were Samuel and her brothers.

The Secret Room

After lunch, the children congregated upstairs in Charles's tower bedroom, far from the adults. Mr MacFarlane had stayed for a meal, before heading back to his farmhouse, and Granny Hughes was tidying and clearing the kitchen. They lounged on Charles's bed, with Sebastian flopped in the chair.

"I still think their bodies are buried in a plague pit somewhere," Samuel said. "That's why Eliza can't really be sure about where their graves are. She just knows they're buried elsewhere."

"But why go to all the fuss of a headstone with their names on it?" Fiona wanted to know.

"They were a well-to-do family. Of course they'd want proper graves and memorial headstones ... to show they loved their children," Charles put in.

"What a morbid subject this is!" Sebastian said, clicking his fingers idly.

"Isn't it?" Fiona said.

"I think it's time we tried to find this secret room

... if there really is one," Charles said, leaping off the bed suddenly. The others followed. He hurried down the stairs and strode off in the direction of the utility room, emerging a few minutes later with a hammer, a chisel and one or two other heavy and lethal-looking tools. Samuel glanced nervously over his shoulder, waiting for Granny or someone to discover them. But no one appeared.

"What are you planning on doing with those?" Fiona asked her brother uneasily, as he stood in the open doorway, weighing them in his hands.

"You'll see," he said.

"Mum is going to kill us," Fiona murmured, not for the first time, as they followed Charles back upstairs to the tower. The spiralling stone staircase resounded to their footfalls, but they tried to be as quiet as possible, so as not to alert the adults.

"This secret room ..." Charles said.

"If there is one," Sebastian interrupted.

"... has to be next door to my room," Charles finished, ignoring his brother.

"Excellent deduction, Sherlock!"

Fiona nudged Sebastian sharply in the ribs.

They stopped outside Charles's bedroom door. He moved along slightly, feeling the wall with his hands.

"A doorway ought to be ... possibly ... round about

... here," he muttered to himself. Then, to everyone's horror and amazement, he picked up his hammer and swung it hard against the wall. The whole staircase seemed to reverberate with the impact.

"Don't you think someone might hear?" Samuel said.

"What if someone comes?" Fiona added.

"We've got time," Charles breathed heavily, as he took another swing. "It has to be done."

As he made another aim for the wall, Charles found himself thinking about his nightmare. If they succeeded in breaking through this wall and finding a secret room on the other side of it, would this make things better or worse? He had no idea, but he knew they had to take the risk. They couldn't give up now. Down in the kitchen, the adults were busy about their separate tasks and didn't hear the noise at first. But after a while, it was impossible to miss. The whole house shuddered and shook with each impact.

Granny and Chris Morton looked at each other in alarm.

"What now?" Chris said. Without saying another word, she began to make her way upstairs.

At the top of the tower, Charles, Sebastian, Samuel and Fiona were banging and crashing with avid determination, swinging tools and attacking the plaster with a vengeance. They were on a mission now and nothing would stand in their way.

Eventually they broke through, just as Chris Morton began to climb the spiralling tower staircase.

With a cry of triumph, they peered through the jagged opening and saw what they had been hoping to find. The hole revealed a secret chamber that had been hidden and bricked-up for four centuries. Debris littered the ground and dust flew through the air, making them cough and splutter. They stepped through into the secret room. They had reached "the other side," no matter how crude and unorthodox their method.

Charles and Samuel tried to wrench open the window shutters. They broke apart in their hands, riddled with damp and rot, and a dim light streamed through the ivy and into the room for the first time in four hundred years, alighting on shelves and ruined books, and a scatter of broken toys on the floor. Spiders and mice scuttled away into corners, and a powder-grey dust lay thick as snow everywhere.

Fiona dipped a finger into it and smelled it.

"It's lime, I think," she said. "Chalk and lime."

"Didn't they used to cover the bodies of the dead with lime?" Samuel asked. "To stop disease from spreading. I read it in that book in the library, when it mentioned the plague ..." His voice trailed away.

There was no one inside the room. No helpless boy crying for his mother, no pale girl ... but there was evidence of their habitation everywhere. There were discarded objects, broken furniture, all draped with cobwebs. Then their eyes alighted upon the most telling detail of all. A group of crudely-carved wooden soldiers lay on the floor. They had been arranged into battle formation, and although one or two of them had toppled over, the rest still held their ground. It seemed that only recently a child had been playing with them.

The four children were instantly silenced, the realization of what they could see flooding through every corner of their minds. They had found their two little ghost children.

Chris Morton now stood in the broken-down opening behind them, rubble and lath and plaster littered all about her feet.

"What on *earth* do you think you are doing?" she asked slowly, staring at them.

By way of an answer, they moved aside, pointing to the scene within the secret chamber.

Chris Morton gets a Shock

Chris Morton stared in amazement at what the children had uncovered: the toys, the beds ... evidence of habitation everywhere.

"My goodness," she breathed quietly, on a sigh. "My goodness me!"

Finally, she found her voice. "All this time, the house has hidden a secret room, and we never knew it was here."

The four children gazed at her in silence. Seeing the little soldiers brought it home to them.

"This is ..." she hesitated, trying to find the right words. "This is quite something. We ought to think about contacting someone ... telling them about it. Historic Scotland, maybe."

"Do we really want other people tramping about the place, poking their noses in?" Charles said.

"But it's history ... it's evidence ..." she murmured.

"Evidence of what? Of cruelty against children in 1604!" Fiona exploded.

Everyone glanced at her in surprise. "Well ... it's true! They were left here to die." Fiona was unapologetic.

"No one could help it. Their mother probably had no choice," Samuel said.

"Wait a minute, wait a minute," Chris Morton said. "What's 1604 got to do with anything? Are you saying you know something about the children who slept in this room? In all this decay and filth?"

The children looked sheepish. "We've been meaning to tell you" Fiona began "... but we were afraid to."

Their mother gazed sternly at them all. "Well now's your chance. Fill me in," she commanded. And so they began to tell their story, of what they knew so far.

"And it's all led to this," Mrs Morton sighed, unable to believe the evidence of her own eyes. "This terrible room, with its ..." she turned her back on it.

"I need time to think," she added. "There's an awful lot to take in."

Chris Morton ordered the children downstairs. She would deal with the mess later. Once they had gone, she strode into the library, a room she never usually liked to frequent. But now she needed to be on her own. She sat down at her husband's leather-topped desk and gazed at the bookshelves. What nightmare had been enacted within these walls that she called home? What was she to do? Was it time to move on, at last?

She gazed up at the gloomy portraits of her husband's ancestors on the walls around her. They offered no help. Then her eye alighted on the framed tapestry, the sampler which Catherine Morton had stitched. She looked at it for a long time. Then she tucked it beneath her arm and made as if to leave.

She passed through the drawing room, but when she got to the landing outside her own room, she froze.

Two children had appeared at the end of the corridor, a boy and a girl, standing side by side. She had time to observe that they were holding hands and that their feet were bare. They stared at Chris Morton as if in entreaty ... as if demanding something of her, but she did not know what it was. She had never seen them before. This was the first time. And, unbeknown to her, would be the last. It was a while before anyone moved. Then, almost imperceptibly, the children faded away and were gone.

Clutching the framed tapestry to her, she hurried down the staircase. The others were gathered in the kitchen, telling Granny Hughes about their discovery of the secret room upstairs.

Chris Morton hesitated outside the door before deciding to join them. She remembered the curse of Catherine Morton and the trouble they had been through last winter.

She had made her decision. It was time to leave Dunadd behind. She would let everyone know as soon as possible.

Down in the basement, it was dark and eerie. Mr Hughes, with the help of Charles, was attempting to see if anything could be done about the dodgy state of the electricity. They located the power box, and Mr Hughes shook his head sagely.

"Just as I thought," he murmured. "A loose connection." After more minutes of tinkering, with Charles holding a torch for him, the problem seemed to be resolved. "You know this wiring's faulty," Mr Hughes added. "She should get it seen to." He pulled down a lever. Instantly, the house was flooded with light. They heard a cheer coming from above.

"That's pleased everyone," Mr Hughes grinned.

The huge building buzzed into life and blazed with unaccustomed light. The boiler fired up, the radiators started ticking, TVs and radios began to mutter all over the house.

Chris Morton heard a happy, triumphant yell coming from the kitchen.

"Hurray," someone bellowed.

By the time she joined them they were already celebrating, unaware that things were about to change forever.

Running Away

"But why?" Fiona protested, glaring at her mother and fighting to hold back the tears.

"Why?" her mother repeated. "Because I've seen those children for myself ... just like you have!"

"I know that, but shouldn't we find out what happened to them?" Fiona cried.

"I *dread* to think what happened to them," Chris Morton said quietly.

She would not be drawn any further on the subject.

"It's been a hard decision to make, but I believe it's a sensible one ... under the circumstances."

She sounds like a politician, Fiona thought bitterly.

Granny Hughes said nothing. She stood at the kitchen sink, wondering how she would cope without life up at Dunadd House. It was certainly time for her and Jim to take a rest from all the hard work, but there was no doubt about it, she would miss the place. And she would miss the children. She'd known them since they were babies. Her throat constricted at the thought of it, and she could hardly bring herself to look at Mrs Morton. Mr Hughes would be devastated when she told him. She had not dared to do so yet. He was out chopping wood in the barn, loading it onto the back of the trailer. His heart would be broken when she told him. The two of them would be lost without Dunadd, in spite of its ghosts.

She had been right after all then. Granny had always suspected that this place was cursed. She'd felt it in her bones.

Fiona stormed off next door to find Samuel.

"What?" he gazed at her open-mouthed when she told him. His heart sank. "You're all leaving?"

She nodded grimly.

His mother stood behind them, listening. So the Mortons were finally going to leave Dunadd. If they *were* leaving, Isabel thought to herself philosophically, then there was certainly no future for herself and Samuel here.

Without saying anything, she left the two children to their private commiserations and wandered across the courtyard to the barn. She pushed the door open onto the dusty silence and ran her hand along the worktops. She had put so much effort into creating this space for herself. *All I need is an empty room,* she thought. But she would miss working here in the old barn on Sheriffmuir, listening to the wind nudging at the door and looking out of the small window at the bare trees and the looming tower of Dunadd.

Just then the door was pushed open and Chris Morton appeared.

"Isabel, I have some news I thought you should know."

"I've just heard," Isabel said. "The children were talking."

"Oh, I see ..." Chris Morton looked apologetic. "I *am* sorry. I know how happy you and Samuel have been here, but I know it's the right thing to do. I can't risk anything else happening to my sons. I'm sure you feel the same way about Samuel."

Isabel nodded.

"I'm going to make arrangements as soon as possible and then put the house on the market. That should hopefully give you enough time to find other accommodation."

Isabel was silent. She didn't relish the prospect of living on in the cottage while the huge house next door stood empty. It would be very strange indeed. She would have to look into it right away. As soon as the snow began to melt. Her heart felt heavy as she put things into boxes and jars. *Might as well make a start*, she reasoned, trying to remain positive.

Farewells

After the discovery of the secret room, the two child spirits had kept their distance.

Everyone had made a concerted effort to tidy up the mess resulting from Charles's brutal assault on the brickwork; they swept up the dust and debris, trying to leave the offending area as clean as possible. Sometimes, one or other of them would drift upstairs, into the exposed inner chamber that had lurked within the tower for four centuries. It was difficult to believe that it had always been there.

Fiona went to the window, peering through the ivy and the broken shutters at the scene below. Light had entered this room for the first time in four hundred years, and the objects inside it were only just beginning to adjust to the intrusion. Spiders and mice no longer made it their home. Eliza and John had not been seen since. *What had happened to them?* Fiona wondered. *Where had they gone?*

Inspecting John's wooden soldiers made her sad. She

wanted to give him something back, so she had asked her brothers for some of their old toys. They gathered together a pirate ship and some tiny model figures and left them in the centre of the room. In addition, Fiona had retrieved an old satin party dress from the back of her wardrobe, knowing it would fit Eliza perfectly. She took it upstairs and laid it on one of the beds, which had been brushed and swept clean of both cobwebs and dirt. *What would they make of their gifts?*

The snow had gone and both families were counting the days before it was time to say their farewells. It was a difficult period for all of them ... unsettling, to say the least.

Packing cases and crates filled the hallway, and Samuel skirted his way around them in search of Fiona. She was sitting halfway up the stairs, her head in her hands.

"We can keep in touch," he said, nudging her.

She didn't speak at first.

"That's not the point," she muttered. "The boys and I were born here. How can we leave it behind?"

Samuel slid onto the step below her.

"You're right," he said. "I've only lived here a year, but I'm still going to miss it. I can't believe it."

"Neither can I."

"Why is she being so stubborn?" Fiona cried. "She

just goes ahead and makes a decision that affects us all without even asking us. How come adults have all the power?"

"Because they think they know what's best for us," he suggested.

"Well they don't ... especially not in this case."

"We can't let it happen," Fiona protested. She was sitting with her brothers in their father's old library.

"We have to," Charles told her. "You have to accept it. There's nothing we can do about it."

"It's like Mum said," Sebastian added. "When we're adults we can make up our own minds about where we're going to live. But until then ..."

"Why are you two so ready to give up? Why can't you make a fuss?"

"What's the point?" Sebastian sighed.

"There's every point in the world," Fiona burst out. "Because of this," she slammed her fist down on their father's old desk, "and because of this ..." She swept her hand round at the books and pictures lining the walls.

"They're just *things*," Charles said. "We can take them with us."

"I'm not talking about things. I'm talking about history. Family history. A sense of place. A sense of belonging. We can't take that with us."

Eliza Morton was watching all of this from the shadows, vaguely impressed. There was more to her descendant, Fiona, than met the eye.

She fingered the pretty shiny dress that Fiona had left out for her. She had looked upon it with scorn, at first, refusing to wear it. John played with his pirate ship and all the little figures, murmuring to himself in peaceful contentment, but she had promised herself she would not be bought as easily as that.

But gradually she had gazed at the dress, touching the material occasionally, stroking its satin smoothness. And in the end, she had put it on.

"A dress for me. A pirate ship for you," she had whispered softly.

Fiona could not hear her.

Eliza Morton giggled to herself, as if thinking of a private joke.

She drifted off, in search of her brother. He was often hiding these days, making himself so thin and flat that not even *she* could always make out the increasingly faint outline of him. He had a knack of merging into the background.

Eliza wanted to keep an eye on Chris Morton before the family left for good, and she wanted her brother to help her. The two of them would watch Mrs Morton, dog her every move.

John Morton tries to talk

"What is it Samuel?" Isabel asked, watching her son pack up his few remaining belongings into the box marked SAMUEL'S ROOM. He had filled that crate in Edinburgh just over a year ago, in order to come and live here, on Sheriffmuir. One year on and they were nomads once again.

Samuel didn't look at her. He had his back turned. She wondered if he blamed her.

"I was happy here," Samuel admitted. "I don't want to leave."

"I know you don't. And surprisingly enough … neither do I."

"She's made up her mind though."

"Looks like it."

"Why can't things ever stay the same?" he asked.

"I don't know, Samuel."

"Life always gets messed up in the end."

"Not always," she added, putting a hand on his shoulder.

"It's easy for you to say. You're an adult. You can go wherever you like," he complained.

"Is that what you think?"

She looked at his few things scattered about. She could see why he would miss it. She would too. The cottage had become theirs. She would miss relaxing on the sofa at night, listening to the murmur of the Wharry Burn through the window, or the breeze sighing in the trees. She loved it here as much as he did.

"It's not quite like that," Isabel said.

"What's not?"

"Adults can't always go where they want."

"It feels like it."

"I can't always control things. I wish I could. The cottage isn't mine. I have to leave it, if the Mortons are leaving."

He said nothing, but threw another book onto the pile in the crate.

Fiona caught up with him later. He was looking gloomy. He already felt as if the others were distancing themselves from him, making ready for their departure. They were going to stay with an aunt in Argyll, while preparing the house and estate for selling.

"It's just a small cottage she's got on the estate, so we won't be living in a big house or anything. But I think that might be quite nice in a way." She was trying to put a brave face on it.

"Granny and Mr Hughes are still going to come up to Dunadd sometimes, to keep an eye on the place while it's empty," Fiona continued.

"Oh good." He wondered if this was supposed to be a comfort to him.

"I'll email you every day," she said.

He nodded.

"You can come and stay sometimes, if you like. Mum said that would be fine."

He nodded again.

"Don't be so glum." She nudged him affectionately. "Nothing will stop us from being friends. Not you and me."

He smiled, taking courage. "You're right," he said. "I just wish ..." He couldn't trust himself to continue. His life at Dunadd during the past year was beyond anything he could ever have imagined happening in his life. He would never forget it. Never. He wanted every detail about Dunadd to be imprinted and scorched on his mind forever.

"We're only taking a few things at first," Fiona said. "Essentials and stuff. Until we find somewhere else to live. Permanently I mean."

"Who would have believed it ... the Mortons leaving after all this time," Samuel murmured.

"I know," Fiona said. "Hard to believe, isn't it. I wonder how the house will feel without us."

Outside the moon gave off a light so bright that the shadows of things stood out clearly: the greenhouse; an abandoned wheelbarrow filled with ice and dead leaves; places where no one would go again; objects no one would pick up, except to tidy away or discard ... not to use.

Later that night, the four sat watching television in the downstairs room next to the kitchen. It was the scruffiest room in the house ... and the coldest. They'd pulled blankets over themselves to keep out the chill and huddled close together for comfort.

Suddenly the television reception went fuzzy, black and white snow fizzing across the screen.

"Hey, I was watching that," Sebastian cried. "Who's got the remote?"

"Not me," Fiona said.

Then she turned her head slowly. A strange and solemn little figure had come to stand quietly behind Samuel's chair.

"Samuel," she whispered, her face ashen.

"What? What is it?"

She nodded her head and he glanced over his shoulder.

John Morton stood there in silence, his small pale face distressed. His cheek bones were thin and hollow, his eyes dark and sad and Fiona felt instantly sorry for him; this sad little boy, who slept upstairs among the cobwebs and relied on his sister for company.

They all looked at him, waiting for him to speak.

"It wasn't our mother," he whispered.

No one said anything.

"She did not do anything wrong."

There was an awful silence as Fiona considered what to say. The boys were all speechless, hopeless in a crisis.

"No one is saying that she did," she murmured, looking at him carefully.

Suddenly another dark figure loomed in the shadows behind him.

"What are you telling them?" Eliza whispered fiercely.

"I wasn't. I was just ..." He sounded pitiful and sad.

"Be quiet," she said crossly.

Fiona glanced at the scared little boy, feeling sorrier than ever.

Eliza Morton had John by the hand now and was

leading him away. He was beginning to fade, to grow thinner and fainter.

"Wait!" Fiona cried, willing them to stop. "What happened to you? Who put you in that room?" But Eliza dragged him out of the light into the shadows of the passageway outside.

"It was not her fault. They made her do it."

It was a faint whisper only, but they all heard his voice clearly just before he disappeared.

Memories

The large house creaked and moaned all about them, as if conscious that huge changes were imminent. The family were asleep in their beds. Boxes and suitcases were half-packed in hallways and corridors. The mahogany grandfather clock that had marked time for two hundred years, ticked away the remaining hours relentlessly. Tomorrow was the day they had all been dreading. The Mortons would pack up and abandon the house for good, leaving Granny Hughes and her husband to supervise the place in their absence. After this, Samuel and his mother would slowly prepare to leave. They had another few days left. Isabel had contacted a friend in Edinburgh and they were going to stay in her flat for a while.

Samuel was broken-hearted. He'd become used to the open landscape, the trees, the murmuring Wharry Burn, the hills. He couldn't imagine being cooped up in the city again.

The only voices to echo here would be the voices of ghost children, looking for an absent mother.

Now the house waited for them to leave.

"I am frightened," John whispered again.

"You are always frightened."

The barely visible figures slowly circled the dark spiralling staircase until they came to rest outside one door in particular.

Eliza Morton's eyes gleamed.

"I like this not at all," John murmured.

"Hush!" She silenced him with a glance.

They crept through the narrow gap in the doorway and stood looking across at the four-poster bed. Chris Morton was sleeping soundly. Despite her fears and anxieties she had had no trouble in falling asleep tonight. Exhaustion had claimed her entirely. She was completely unaware of the room around her and of the two figures who crept ever closer to her bed ...

They stood looking down at her sleeping peacefully. Eliza held her candle aloft, the light from it flickering dimly over the bed.

"I wish we had a mother," John wailed softly.

"We did have a mother," Eliza replied. "She abandoned us."

"She did not," John protested, rounding on her. "I remember what happened ... and she never meant to leave us. She was broken-hearted."

Buried memories resurfaced from the long distant past as they remembered how they had first got sick.

No one in the house at Dunadd was suffering from the plague. There had been isolated incidents reported as far afield as Stirling and Alloa, but no one up here on the estate had succumbed, where the air was clean. Their parents had felt secure in this knowledge ... until John took ill, very suddenly.

At first, they thought it was nothing worse than a common cold, but then the bruises and swellings started to appear. Their mother watched in horror, refusing to believe the truth. Although their parents were wealthy, the children, John and Eliza, had always lived in fear of the household staff. They knew that no one would help them or be kind to them, so when Eliza fell sick as well, it was their mother who nursed them.

The servants told her she should not do so; that she would catch the disease herself and die. But she refused to listen. She would not abandon her children in their hour of distress. She wiped and bathed their little bodies, sat with them as they suffered. Their mother cared not about contracting the disease as well. But she remained untouched. Throughout the course of their illness – which lasted a matter of days – she stayed fit and healthy, nursing them until they were dead. Then she sat in the little room where they died, refusing to move. The fetid air bothered her not one bit, despite the protestations of her husband and the servants. She would not budge.

"It is not safe to touch the bodies," she was told.

"They will be buried in a decent burial ground," their mother insisted, as finally she was taken to her own room to rest, sitting in silence for hours until at last she began to weep and mourn.

Unbeknown to her, her instructions were ignored. Lime was spread around the room, on the beds and the floors, and the children were put into sacks and thrown into a communal grave: a plague pit on the other side of the hill, near Alloa.

Two headstones were erected in the graveyard on the edge of the moor, down by the little chapel where their mother sometimes had worshipped with her children. No one but their father and the priest knew that the graves were empty; that their bodies lay elsewhere. Their mother was never told the truth. Her husband constructed a convenient web of lies. He wanted to offer her comfort, that was all, and he knew that two little memorial stones were the only comfort she would have.

The empty room was sealed up on the advice of all.

The servants and staff were glad when every trace of the room was removed, knowing they had treated the children badly at times, especially in the last days of their illness. They had refused to help them, or give them so much as a sip of water. They were too terrified of the plague.

But their mother had not been afraid. Disobeying her husband, she had gone to her children's aid.

Houses keep hold of their memories. It was a long time before the bricked-up room ceased to be remembered, and became a secret truly kept. Finally, there was no one left living who remembered. The secret room remained a secret, until four children began to probe and pry ...

"Don't you remember?" John persisted bravely, working on his sister. "She had no choice. She nursed us until we were dead. Everyone told her that she must seal up the room afterwards."

There was a slight softening of Eliza's face as she listened to her brother's words. "They said the bodies were not safe to touch."

"That is right, Eliza. You remember now?"

In their minds, the two children could hear their mother's distraught cries as if it was only yesterday. Four hundred years had intervened, but her love for them had never faded or gone away.

"They forced her to," John muttered. "They said it was the right thing to do. They sprinkled grey powder everywhere, all over our bodies and the beds and furniture, before they took us away to the pit. Then they bricked it up. But she wailed and wailed."

Eliza looked at her little brother with dawning realisation. "You are right. Now I remember. Now I understand."

"None of this is *their* mother's fault," he added, looking down at the woman sleeping in the bed before them. And taking his older sister by the hand, he led her quietly from the room.

Chris Morton slept on, suspecting not a thing.

Escape

Charles sat up, sweating. He'd had his nightmare again, the one about the house becoming a burnt-out ruin, himself gliding above it, able to see clearly inside. A roofless ruin with snow drifting in. In the distance, he could hear dogs barking; yelping and howling as if their lives depended on it. The dogs invaded his sleep. He woke up.

Remembering his dream, he looked up and saw with relief that the ceiling was still in place.

He flopped back onto the mattress and closed his eyes. Then he opened them again. Why *were* the dogs making all that noise?

Something was roaring on the floor below.

And he could smell something ... something acrid, catching at the back of his throat. Smoke!

He leapt from his room in an instant, calling out the names of his brother and sister as he ran.

Sebastian appeared immediately from his room, having also been roused by the barking. Together, they stumbled down the narrow tower staircase, clutching at each other in the darkness. On the floor below, smoke billowed and filled the air, making them choke and splutter, so that it was almost impossible to see ahead. The dogs' barking was more incessant now. They must have woken him in the first place, Charles realized, although he was too preoccupied to think of this. All he could think about was escaping from the terrible inferno that their house had become.

On reaching Fiona's bedroom, they found the door wide open and no one inside. A terrible crackling sound surrounded them. Still clutching at each other, they tried to make their way to the staircase, but were stopped in their tracks by a beam falling across their path, a burning timber which smashed sideways, trapping them where they were. For a moment, Sebastian hesitated, cowering in the darkness, too afraid to move. Charles, understanding that his brother was in shock, shook him, forcing him down onto his knees. It took some time before Sebastian realized what was being asked of him.

"Crawl," Charles ordered. "Crawl on your knees."

With no other option, they slithered below the fallen beam, managing to avoid the worst of the smoke. The air at floor level was cleaner, easier to breathe. As they passed their mother's room, they saw orange flames licking the curtains, running up and down them like quicksilver, eating them alive. Like Fiona's bedroom, it, too, was empty.

The fire was like a living, breathing monster, swallowing all in its path: a voracious animal that would stop at nothing. It was a force beyond them. They couldn't hope to win this battle ... only struggle to escape. They crawled their way down the stairs, in time to see another beam come crashing down on the floor above, ruining their home, their house ... everything they held dear. Sebastian was crying, his breath coming in gasps now. They had no idea where the others were; if they were still alive, or if they were trapped somewhere inside the flames.

"Where are they?" Sebastian sobbed.

"Keep going," Charles begged. "Just keep going," and he dragged his brother behind him, mindful of the blinding smoke that was thickening all about them with every passing second. The roar of the fire was deafening as they crawled on all fours away from the foot of the spiral staircase, shouting for their mother and Fiona as they went. Their hearts felt as if they were bursting from their chests. The grandfather clock stood where it had always stood, flat against the wall in the shadows, the last thing to burn ... but it too would perish.

Everything in the world that they owned was now a huge conflagration, a bonfire that lit up the sky for miles around.

At the Sheriffmuir Inn they saw it. Even Mr MacFarlane down at Lynns Farm saw the orange glow above the treetops.

Once on the ground floor, the boys found their way to the kitchen and the outer door blocked by falling debris and swirling, choking flames. They had to find another way out. In the hallway, not far from the grandfather clock, was a grander, more formal-looking front door which was never used. Hidden behind a thick velvet curtain, it was so rarely breached that they mostly forgot it existed. They tried to open this now. However, through disuse, the bolts had rusted and it took several tense moments of jiggling and panicky brute force until they finally slid across and the key turned in the lock.

They threw the door open just as a whole interior panel came crashing down behind them.

Stepping into the night, the cold air hit them in stark contrast to the blazing inferno from which they'd just escaped. Coughing and spluttering, they staggered clear of the flames, and lay prone on the frosty ground, sucking clean air into their lungs.

Sebastian was sobbing with the effort. Charles put an arm round his brother's shoulder.

"Where are they?" Sebastian cried. "Where are the others?"

Charles said nothing. He did not know the answer to that question. Instead they sat in silence, catching their breath, watching their home burn.

Suddenly, in the darkness, Charles became aware of movement to the left of them and with immense relief saw figures huddled in a group and their sister running towards them, sobbing.

"We thought you were trapped," she cried, grabbing at them both hysterically. "We thought you were trapped in the tower."

The children gathered with Granny Hughes and her husband at the front of the building, watching the flames leap. Fiona was being comforted by Granny, who in turn was inconsolable. No one knew where Chris Morton was. No one had seen her.

Samuel and his mother appeared and ran across to join them, and they all stared helplessly as the fire tore through Dunadd, eating up carpets and curtains, swallowing tables and chairs, devouring everything in its path.

Everyone had the same thought. Charles was trembling. *Where was their mother?*

The fire service had been called by the watchers at

Sheriffmuir Inn and was on its way but Sheriffmuir was an isolated place to get to. In the meantime, they had to watch their home burn.

"There she is. There," cried Fiona, running towards a darkened figure, which had emerged from the side of the building, bent double and coughing, clutching something in her hand and preceded by barking dogs.

"Oh, thank God. You're all safe," Chris Morton whispered hoarsely, clutching her children to her.

She and Isabel stood side by side, the children huddled close. Soot and debris peppered the snow, which had gradually thawed over the past few days. At least the fire service would be able to access the moor; something which would not have been possible just a few days before.

Fiona grabbed her mother's arm, and the boys gazed at their mother with wide-eyed relief. She was safe. For a few moments they had imagined the worst, but she was there before them, unharmed. Their mother. At times she annoyed them and they her, but life without each other was unthinkable ... untenable.

As the great house before them crackled and roared, Chris Morton glanced around.

This is what is important, she thought, looking at the people gathered about her. *Not a stupid old house ... but this.*

The two families leaned close together for comfort, and watched Dunadd burn.

Flames leaped and roared, devouring the rafters, the turrets and the tower, leaving a blackened corpse, almost unrecognizable in its devastation. Dunadd House had stood upon the moor for nearly five centuries. Now, a roofless ruin would take its place – just as in Charles's dream. A shiver ran down his spine as he stood there in the cold, surrounded by his family and friends whom he loved, in spite of their differences, and in spite of the history that had hounded them all their lives.

Skull and Crossbones

It was a miracle that no one had even suffered from smoke inhalation. The exact cause of the fire remained unknown. Fire inspectors suspected that the wiring had been faulty for years and in need of repair, and was probably the cause of the blaze.

Others could confirm this, particularly Charles and Mr Hughes who had examined the power box in the basement. The electricity had been temperamental in recent days, to say the least.

They spent the night – their final night – all sleeping on sofas and chairs in Samuel's cramped little cottage, Granny Hughes and her husband included. It was a terrible squash, but no one minded. None of them could quite believe what had happened. They were suffering from shock.

"It's a mercy none of us were hurt, so it is," Granny kept muttering.

The smell of smoke and charred remains drifted

across the courtyard. The shell of the house remained. It could be rebuilt ... but at a cost.

Fiona thought sadly about the grandfather clock, the grand piano, the paintings and family heirlooms, the antiques, the books ... not to mention the rabbit that had perished in the flames. The dogs had escaped with Mrs Morton. In fact it was the dogs that had saved them. As soon as they had smelled the flames, they had barked and barked to raise the alarm.

Chris Morton was thinking about the insurance. Nothing could replace what they had lost, but she reminded herself that they could have lost an awful lot more.

As they sat drinking tea by the roaring stove, the adults comforted each other with stories and memories about the past. A warm feeling emanated from them all, despite the terrible circumstances of their plight.

"I wonder how the fire *did* start?" Fiona whispered to Samuel, as she hugged her knees quietly in the shadows next to the stove.

He shrugged his shoulders, but both wondered if Eliza and John Morton may have had something to do with it. They could not have been more wrong.

"We've lost so much," Granny was wailing.

Chris Morton shook her head sadly. "I always found

it a burden, to be honest," she admitted, although she did feel desperately sad at the thought of all their belongings; valuables, which had been in the family for generations, had all been wiped out in a single night. "There's something liberating about starting again, from scratch. After all, we come into this world with nothing ..."

Granny Hughes rolled her eyes. "That'll be the shock talking," she barked.

"Well, whatever it is, I managed to rescue one thing. This."

She held up the framed tapestry that had hung in the library: the sampler of the two children standing beside the tower.

"Why?" Granny Hughes said, staring at it in astonishment. It was a poultry little treasure to have rescued, in Granny's eyes.

Chris Morton shook her head. "I don't really know why. It was signed by Catherine Morton herself. Maybe that's it ..."

Fiona reached for the tapestry and stared at the distorted stitches, delicately and neatly executed by Catherine Morton, when she was incarcerated in her own house at the end of her life.

"I noticed something else too," Chris Morton surprised them all by saying.

"What?"

"You'll need good eyesight."

"I've got a magnifying glass if that'll help," Samuel cried. "It's packed already, but I might be able to reach it at the top of the box."

He disappeared and returned a few minutes later.

Chris Morton held the magnifying glass over the picture and they took turns at peering at the minute stitches. There was an emblem embroidered into the body of the tower.

"A skull and crossbones," Fiona breathed. "It's tiny."

Samuel's jaw dropped open. "It's a symbol of the plague! That confirms what we thought all along."

Fiona and Samuel both grew pale. Both were thinking of the hollowed-out eyes of the two ghost children, John and Eliza Morton.

"They died of the plague," Fiona said in a small voice. "And they blamed their mother for abandoning them to it. There would have been nothing she could do."

Then the ultimate horror occurred to them. That's why the room had been sealed off. It was believed to have been contaminated by the plague. In those days, there was nothing anyone could do for the victims. Anyone approaching them, or trying to help, would probably have contracted the plague and died too. So the room had been sealed off and bricked-up eventually. No one wanted to remember. Everyone wanted to forget.

But not their mother. She never forgot.

Isabel shuddered. "I think it's about time we all had a milky drink. I don't know about the rest of you, but I can't sleep yet."

"This cottage to rent on my sister's farm ..." Chris said speculatively, glancing towards Isabel, "... there are two of them actually." Samuel's ears pricked up. "I don't suppose you'd consider renting the other one?"

Isabel glanced briefly at Samuel then smiled. "We'd love to."

Fiona sat up and flung her arms round her mother.

"We can start again," she said. "I know we can."

"Five hundred years is a lot of time to make up for," Chris Morton warned, thinking of the house and everything they had lost.

But Fiona felt as if she could face anything, as long as she had her family and Samuel by her side.

Epilogue

That summer a new sign was hammered up next to the wooden gate at the bottom of the drive.

FOR SALE

Whoever bought this property would have to start completely from scratch.

And would they have heard the rumours of a couple of ghost children found in a sealed-off room? Stories had been told. Some of them true.

The spiralling staircase lay open to the sky – just as in Charles's dream – and if you looked very carefully, it was said that you could see two pale children standing in the ruins. They vanished and re-appeared. Vanished and re-appeared. No one was really sure if they were there ...

Dunadd House, as a ruin, had acquired a far worse

reputation than it ever had when it was occupied. But maybe one day someone would claim it and take care of it. Otherwise, it would remain a wreck, slowly deteriorating with time.

Mr MacFarlane walked up there sometimes, and occasionally thought that he glimpsed children among the charred remains. He wondered if the place would ever be sold.

"I wouldn't buy it," he muttered to himself, walking on. "Ghosts are best left to themselves."

In the distance, something shimmered. Dressed unaccustomedly in a beautiful satin dress, Eliza smiled at her brother John.

"Come," she said. "None shall harm us now."

Then, taking each other's hands, they drifted across the broken ruins, fading back into the walls of their home, to live with their memories.

Alex Nye

Scottish Children's Book Award winner

Delve deeper into Dunadd's secrets –
read on for an eerie extract from *Chill*,
the spine-tingling prequel to *Shiver*.

Samuel was alone in the house. Outside the moor lay silent, stretching away into endless emptiness. Dunadd was completely deserted. He liked it this way, having the place entirely to himself. He could almost pretend the house was his. There was an atmosphere of secrecy and silence, which grew more intense when there was no one else about. The others had all gone skiing – it was all they could think to do on the snowbound moor. The drifts were so high that the narrow winding road, which led up to the isolated Dunadd House, had become impassable.

It was so quiet. There was nothing but the sound of the wind in the trees, and the distant murmur of the Wharry Burn, water travelling and rumbling beneath ice. The whole moor was covered with snow, an ocean of unending white, waves of it packed up against the walls of the barn and cottage – the cottage where Samuel now lived.

The rooms, corridors and staircases of Dunadd House creaked all about him in the silence. Numerous empty rooms lay behind heavy oak doors.

Samuel had felt nervous as he crossed the snowy courtyard, the white tower looming above him, but he was not going to be put off. He made his way up the silent staircase to the drawing room on the first floor.

The grandfather clock ticked noisily in the hall below, a deep sombre note befitting its age, like the heartbeat of the house itself; constant, regular, marking time.

On the wide landing dark wooden doors concealed their secrets from him, but ahead of him one door stood open. He made his way towards it over the polished boards and Turkish carpets. He trod softly, afraid to disturb the peace. The colours of the rugs were beautiful, tawny-red, crimson and tan-coloured, like the flanks and hide of a red deer. The walls were panelled in dark oak, and he was conscious that above and behind him lay another narrower stone staircase, leading into the tower, a place he had never before explored.

He passed shelves of books, old thumbed paperbacks, family favourites, and pushed open the door at the end. Before him lay the drawing room on the first floor, a vast expanse filled with light from the large bay windows on either side. Old pieces of antique furniture stood about in the shadows, gathering dust.

After a week of raging blizzards the moor had at last fallen silent, and sunlight sparkled and reflected from the snow outside, and reached into the dark corners of the house. Dust motes circulated slowly.

Samuel was familiar with this room. He had been here before, most memorably on Christmas Day, just over a week ago, although he preferred not to think about that right now. It only made him nervous, and he didn't want that. He wanted to be able to explore the house, unafraid, without feeling the need to keep glancing back over his shoulder.

He advanced slowly into the centre of the room.

Near the door stood the grand piano, as expected, its lid open and ready to play. Family photographs of the widowed Mrs Morton and her three children stood on its polished surface. At the other end of the room was a massive stone fireplace, its hearth stacked with firewood, unlit at the moment. Mr Hughes would light it later when the family returned. Above the fireplace hung the mirror, framed in elaborate scrolling gilt. Samuel made a deliberate effort not to look into it. He repeatedly drew his eyes away on purpose, especially after what he had last seen there. He didn't want that vision to disturb his dreams again.

He wanted normality, nothing unusual to happen. Or did he? Perhaps he was seeking her out again.

He walked across the drawing room to the window seat on the far side, and sat down with his back to the room. He made himself comfortable and studied the view of the mountains. It was a breathtaking panorama. The whole moor lay beneath him.

He turned his attention to the map underneath the window, a long map of the Highland line, browned with age at the edges, fixed and preserved behind glass. This is what he was here for, ostensibly, to copy the drawing of this map, so that he could have one for his own room. His bedroom in the cottage across the courtyard shared the same view. Mrs Morton had been reluctant to leave him alone in the house at first, but at last she had agreed, and now here he was.

He placed his pens and pencils on a small occasional table and dragged this into position next to him. Then he rolled out his long piece of paper, selected specially for the purpose, and pinned it down onto the table with a weight at either end to stop it from curling inwards.

The oak panelling creaked now and then in the silence, and from a long way away, if he strained his ears, Samuel could still hear the regular, soothing beat of the clock downstairs. He began to draw, his fingers moving rapidly over the paper, his back to the mirror and whatever visions it might contain.

This is an ordinary house, he told himself. *It's old and beautiful and very large, but it holds no sinister secrets.* He almost believed it for a moment.

There was nothing Samuel loved more than copying

maps. He liked drawings with lots of fine lines and detail. It was a gift he'd always had. Even as a small child, sitting in front of the television, he had arranged his pens and pencils in neat rows and would draw away with utter contentment for hours.

As he worked he glanced over his shoulder from time to time at the empty room behind him. The mirror over the mantelpiece remained blank, nothing moved or stirred in its silvery depths.

He stopped drawing and listened. He thought he'd heard a sound on the staircase. The empty house waited, no sound apart from the distant tick of the grandfather clock and Samuel's own breathing. There it was again – a light tread on the stair. He decided it was probably Granny Hughes doing her dusting again, despite the fact she had been ordered to rest by Mrs Morton. She often crept about like that, duster in hand, trying to be invisible in spite of her mutterings and groanings.

He turned back to his drawing, his hand poised over the paper, and began to draw a long curving line, more slowly this time, his ear cocked for any sound outside.

Behind him the door swung slowly inwards – he could feel the draught of it at his back travelling across the room. Slowly he turned his head, but there was no one there.

Then he heard it.

It was the sound of a woman crying. It filled the room around him, permeating the walls and furniture. A bottled-up sound, trapped, as if echoing along a long dark corridor.

Samuel looked about him, spinning this way and that, but the drawing room was empty. Then he heard her footsteps. She passed through the room to the door of the library at the far end. He couldn't see her, but he could hear her footsteps clearly, and the sound of her weeping. Then the library door closed with a bang, and he was left with a terrible silence.

He dashed across the drawing room, stumbling against the furniture in his haste. When he got to the door of the library he rattled the handle furiously, but it was locked ... from the inside. He bent down and peered through the keyhole. The key was still in place. He could see nothing.

He stood up and his eye was caught by the mirror over the fireplace. It reflected back no one but himself.

"I don't believe in ghosts," he whispered to himself. "I don't believe in them." There had to be a logical explanation. *Think with the mind, not the heart.* But his mind was telling him to run.

He fled from the drawing room leaving his pens

and pencils and unfinished map scattered on the window seat. The door swung wide behind him, and he pelted down the staircase, his feet clattering against the wooden boards. He charged along the corridors to the kitchen at the end, calling out for Fiona as he went.

"Fiona? Mrs Hughes?" No one answered him. Granny Hughes was up in her room in the tower, half-asleep, an unread library book on her lap.

He ran outside onto the snow-packed lawn, and stood looking up at the windows on the first floor. The immense panes of glass were dark with shadow. Nothing could be seen in the drawing room. If he closed his eyes he could still hear the sobbing echoing inside his head. He looked all about him at the silent trees, blanketed in snow, the cold bleak hills, hoping to catch a glimpse of Mr Hughes, perhaps busy about his work, or the family returning from their skiing trip, but there was no one. He stared up at the dark mass of the house. Then he thought he saw movement in the library window to the right of the drawing room. A shadow moving, backwards and forwards ... then it was gone.